THE DEADLY SWARM
AND OTHER STORIES

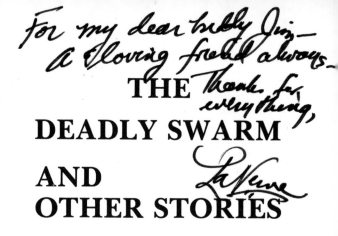

THE DEADLY SWARM AND OTHER STORIES

Written and illustrated by

LaVerne Harrell Clark

Hermes House Press

New York

Grateful acknowledgement is made to the following anthologies and magazines in which these stories first appeared: *Southwest: A Contemporary Anthology*, edited by Karl and Jane Kopp and Bart Lanier Stafford III; *Southwest: Towards the Twenty-First Century*, edited by Karl and Jane Kopp; *Sands: A Literary Review*; and *St. Andrews Review*.

First Edition 1985

Library of Congress Catalog Card Number: 85-61099
ISBN: 0-9605008-2-0

Art Consultant: Susan Lusk

Special thanks to Shirley and Milton Gray and M.E.G. for their editorial assistance

Printed in the United States of America

Hermes House Press, Inc.
127 West 15th Street
New York, NY 10011

This first edition of *The Deadly Swarm and Other Stories*, of which there are seven hundred and fifty copies, was typeset in Baskerville and designed by Richard Mandell in New York City.

For my early writing teachers,
John R. Humphreys and Frances Gillmor,
and with gratitude to those who followed,
especially Vance Bourjaily and Francine Prose

For my husband, L.D.,
whose belief has been unfailing

And finally, for all my long-time
sisters in writing,
particularly Berta Greenwald Ledecky,
Mary Alexander Walker, Byrd Baylor,
Fé McGrail, and Frances Cusack

CONTENTS

The Deadly Swarm

. . . hence with leave
Retiring from the popular noise, I seek
This unfrequented place to find some ease,
Ease to the body some, none to the mind
from restless thoughts, that like a deadly swarm,
Of hornets armed, no sooner found alone,
But rush upon me thronging, and present
Times past, what once I was, and what am now.
   —John Milton, *Samson Agonistes*, 11:15-22

Littleville folks never mentioned ghosts much until the night I came back from the Colorado River with a cracked spine. Afterwards the railroad men talked that I come back to life only halfway. Their women whispered "ghost man" pointing to my paralysis and way of mumbling. I could hear folks saying my mind went stiff with my legs.

They don't notice me much anymore at day. No, not except when I shuffle to the grocery store for a quart of milk. It's at night when they mostly see me—and then it's the black folks and strangers and Main Street people.

The black folks never pass by Old Man

11

Randall's saloon, my Pa's place, now called the Katy Grill by its customers, the railroaders and deadheaders. At night they walk across the street from the beanerie from 7:30 on. They know I'm still sitting in the dark wing of the gallery with my head bowed to the sidewalk. Cutting their eyes across the road, they watch my long fingers running over my tarnished watch fob.

Folks say that I know only the past. I reckon they sense that the present is the jumbled part of a jigsaw puzzle that just doesn't fit together for me. In a way they're right; but still nobody yet has figured me out exactly. Folks can't seem to understand how time can just come to a halt on some folks even while life—a fellow's own and everybody's around him—keeps on. I mean how a fellow like me can come to give up on his outside self just the same as the world has. Yes, and maybe even decide it's for the best because he finds what ease he can that way. Well, maybe that's why while life hums around me like a nest of hornets, I've locked myself outside it and stay fixed to what amounts to a slow motion replay of what in some ways it was once like to be a part of the deadly swarm, and in some ways still is, here in Littleville.

If I could still get my words out clear I

would tell you that my story must have begun the first time Shiny Carson came to the pines along the Crag Rock. She had come alone—a girl of fourteen—and the pines had taken her in like they did me. You might say they had been lonesome while I was away learning at school, for I swear a tree can feel things just the same as any man can. I think those pines had realized that Shiny and me was of their kind. They had known what would happen long before the first time I found her watching me as I swam nude in the early evening, a young fellow, just under twenty.

Though it's always been a favorite spot of mine, folks never came to the Crag Rock much. They was kind of superstitious about it; said it was lonesome like. Every sundown the water below turned from a peaceful day sluggishness into a swirling mass, an infinity of rocky jags, and it scared them off. I had seen it do that since I was a boy and had strung wires from my backyard to the river bank so that I could swing down them like I was on a trolley and be at the circling suction pools near the Rock in no time. I had learned the secret of the place early. I knew it was only the moon through the pines making shadows on the water that made folks notice more in the evening what was going on all day. When the day sounds stopped you could hear the water better. And if there was some things I couldn't explain, I understood them too. Because in a way I felt my own spirit was kind of like the river's.

It's true that ten men's bones lay whirling at the bottom of the suction pools around the mouth of the Crag Rock—it's a big jag of fossil shells that protrudes up from the middle of the Colorado. I've never bothered with ideas of bones much, though. Like the fossil shells along the bank, I figured those bones belonged there too, because they came from men who hadn't understood the river like me and the pines and Shiny did. I've always known why the suction pools was angry, and I could swim them even when I was looped on a quart of Sweet Lucy. My pa, Old Man Randall, had never understood it, though, and he had been after me to keep away from them ever since I had built them trolley lines to reach them when I was a kid.

I remember most of the time that first summer when I had just come home from school and found Shiny on the river. I remember that my classics teacher told me once what Helen and Paris done to Troy. Well, me and Shiny done that same thing in a way to Littleville. Shiny was the kind of girl who the old men said would make a person lay his Bible down. And being the daughter of old Sim Carson, the sheriff, I guess, she was certain to cause quarreling.

Me and the pines and Shiny had felt we was of a kind ever since that first evening together. It was like that all summer with us until old Sheriff Sim caught on when the signs of fall began. Otherwise he'd sent Shiny away quicker to get the bad blood out of her. He'd known Shiny was like her ma, who'd run away with a carnival barker, so when he learned about us, he sent her to a boarding convent, but just a week before Pa sent me back to school. Of course, Old Man Sim was plenty up in the air; he forbade me to ever see Shiny again.

Learning wasn't for me after Shiny, though. So I quit after my Ma and sister died during the flu epidemic and come back here. Pa shouldn't have let me, but I was all he had left so he wanted me home.

Fall was lonesome. What time I wasn't out on the Crag Rock swimming, I was dicing down at Pa's saloon. Mainly waiting for Shiny to come home. Pa was uneasy enough for me. That's why he began to harp on a notion he got from Ma earlier about me marrying. Ma had taken to Cassie Rilkes, the girl who lived down the street from us a piece and who was my special girl in grade school. He began to talk Cassie to me plenty, always telling me how Ma liked to think of us as sweethearts, but mainly I know he thought Cassie was the steadying influence I needed. Cassie's folks had a little money and some plans too, like Pa did. They also seemed to look on Cassie as mine too. I guess they had felt that way from the time I had begun to give her valentines in the second grade, though to tell the truth I can see now that I had put Cassie out of my mind mostly after Shiny reached her early womanhood and came into my life. Anyhow before the year Ma died was out, Pa and Cassie's folks had seen to it that I was taking fragile—she was always kind of fawn-like—Cassie for my own.

I know now I should have shut my ears to Pa's pleas, especially the part that insisted upon how Cassie would steady my life and make it all my folks had once hoped it to be. But at the time I was torn up by the loss of Ma and Sister, and I felt bad too about the way I kept hurting Pa. But above all, it's best I recall the way Shiny's pa kept making me feel hopeless about there being any chance he'd ever let me marry her, much less succeed in carrying her off.

I never looked on Cassie as a real wife though. She seemed to me to be always faraway living a story out; she was like a little girl playing dolls. She was happy enough with her dreams, though, and I had my own world, so we got along just fine.

When Shiny came back, her pa was wedding planning too. His new deputy Rig Lakins was Old Sim's choice, and Rig took to it plenty too. Shiny didn't have any say anyhow. With Rig, her pa, and my pa watching us like hawks it was hard to be together. But gradually we were. Kind of in the background, but everyone felt it and whispered and waited. No one came to the Crag Rock, though, except the Peters' kid who lived next door to me. He was always slying around carrying things back to his Aunt Maidee. Things had begun to look better for me and Shiny too until Shiny's pa had caught her packing her suitcases one night when I was out of town trading cattle. It was then he set the wedding date for her and Rig.

The trouble that had been boiling along, finally busted open that awful August afternoon. I remember being out in back of Pa's saloon playing Big Seven, the best dice game that ever hit Littleville, when Rig Lakins sallied up to watch. I had smelt trouble blowing in on the pine trees and when Rig come up I knew it was time enough it broke. Rig had something up his sleeve that troubled me into stroking my watch fob.

Seeing Rig always made a dirty feeling churn inside me. Maybe it was his name Rig—suited him better, though, than Rigel, his Christian name. Maybe it was the way Rig sallied, sort of lagging his belly over one side of his deputy belt that reminded me of putrid smells like pine souring into resin jelly. Maybe it was the sweat circles under Rig's armpits that did it. But mostly I guess it was the idea of Rig and Shiny together.

Watching Rig standing there, thinking about him with Shiny, feeling the snake eyes in the ivory of the dice, I was ready to leave. I raked the silver on the table into my shirt pocket, letting it tear the starch as it jangled down.

As I brushed past him, Rig was jeering at the pillow cushion I always carried to sit on. I had to level anybody who laughed at my "gambling seat," including Rig. He was laying there knocked out when I turned to look around.

The whole town was gaping at me as I strode past them down to the Crag Rock. But I wasn't feeling except for the snake eyes grinding into my palms.

Soon I was at the river, and the moss and pine shadows and me were all one in the Colorado. Being at the Crag Rock in late afternoon was like being at church to me. The mud slush of the river bottom squeezing through my toes cleaned out my thinking about Rig and the cool spray from over the big jag of rocks lazed my tense fists. I always found home sap there.

Sundown was setting on the jagged rocks and fossil shells, turning them to a glistening when Shiny came that night for our last evening together. It wasn't until middle evening when she left crying; I lay watching the moon spray over the rocks, realizing that it was the first time that I had cried too, and that this new thing she had told me made it worse. It had to be our last evening together.

I went into town and got terrible drunk afterwards. I tried to get past the end of it all by killing a quart of Sweet Lucy. But the stuff didn't help like it had before. And nothing the men in the saloon could say to me would make me let them see me home. I was in a frenzy, so I just stumbled back to the river, where I waited for the past to become this eternity.

After I left the saloon that night, they say my pa came looking for me. They say fear lay in the whites of his eyes. He'd gone to bed sick earlier and had woke up in the night and called for Cassie. She was nearing her time, and he was uneasy for her. When Cassie didn't answer, he'd gone looking for her and found her room empty. So he'd gone next door where Cassie sometimes visited Maidee Peters who was always ailing— Pa knew that Maidee was the only person Cassie ever went around except her folks. Maidee and her sly nephew were newspapers enough for Cassie or anyone else what with their perpetual talk about all that was happening in Littleville. That night when Pa reached Maidee's, she told him that Cassie had been there earlier, but had already left for home.

Folks say that Pa found Cassie and me, though. He ran down the trail back of our house, past the remains of what was once the trolley line. Just before he reached us was when he'd heard that awful sound: two peals of a forty-five among the rocks and fossil shells. Then he saw Maidee's nephew tearing past him like a wild colt, but not before Pa could grab the kid and stop him. Shortly afterwards, Pa found me. Down below the water from the rapids that was washing blood over my face, I was, and still breathing. A little way down past the main whirlpool, Pa found Cassie too. Washed up to the bank, but already lifeless from the bullet in her breast. That night he shook what had happened out of the Peters' boy; the kid was crazed silly from all he'd seen.

Folks didn't again see me moving along the streets—my figure is kind of gaunt and angular and forever caught up in this one pose—until Shiny Carson's boy was five or six. When Old Man Sim Carson saw me moving down the street that first time, I reckon he felt that folks had told him right, for it was then he hushed his talk about killing me. Sim had sworn that since I had come out of everything alive, he would do that for the sake of Shiny's good name. You see, Shiny had left town still unwed after the baby was born, and from then on, folks here only referred to her publicly as "little Sim's mother who was away in the city." Sim raised the boy as his own.

Nowadays when strangers come to Sim with their talk about a funny-looking drunk man on the streets late at night he only walks away. Sim knows strangers don't know it's just me and that I'm sober as I'll ever be. He knows they don't know about the night Cassie, remembering something Maidee Peters let slip, walked out to the Crag Rock and waited for me, her husband, to bring Sim's only daughter there, or how I came alone: drunk.

Strangers would be more confused as to why Rig Lakins shot Cassie when he crept up some distance away and saw her there, standing beside me, begging me to go home with her. Or how the Peters' kid saw Cassie fall from the rocks into the water when the bullet hit with me diving in after her, a second shot whizzing through me. They wouldn't know that Rig realized his mistake too late and threw himself into a suction pool of the river, cursing the Peters' boy as he did so.

But folks do still talk about the Crag Rock, and when they do, they are always sure to end it something like this: "Say, I could of sworn I seen someone a sitting out on the Crag Rock last night when I looked across to it from the bridge. If it wasn't such a spooky idea, I'd of swore it was the young one of . . . Shiny's. My boy tells me that boy's always messing around down at the river just like his . . . well, like his pa used to."

Myself, I'm still not feeling much about the present except for the grinding of some snake eyes into my clenched fists. Yet at midnight, I feel that folks that live along Main Street are often lying awake, just waiting for the familiar scuffing sounds my feet make as I drag them along the sidewalk home. I know folks just sort of expect me in Littleville around that time every night, just like they do the striking of the clock on the court house. I know because, you see, I told you to begin with about how I'm aware that I'm still participating in the deadly swarm of days right here on Main Street in Littleville—mine or anybody's days, and yes, be they past or present.

* * * * * *

Big Damon's Quilt

Old brown trunk, lock all tarnished: to fit a key inside takes a lot of working. Big Damon hammers at the rusty lock: yellow hands pounding time's weir.

Vestal watches: *he'll get it open soon and scoop out pecans. They'll be papershells grown in brown sap.* But it isn't just knowing this, but rather watching him that makes her skin feel tingly. It's really the way he covers those pecans, like they were hidden gold wrapped in his grandmother's quilt. *Her name . . . the one that made that quilt . . . it was Mourning Water, and she's my great-great grandmother: a real Indian too. She sewed that quilt with blue threads, and it's all blue. Big Damon*

27

says she made it for a good luck sign.

"Good old papershells," Big Damon calls, bending over the chest. "Catch'em, kid; they got brittle shells. Yeah, you can crack'em. They ain't too hard for even a li'l mouse."

Big Damon pads to the cowhide chair. Sound: lone and heavy like a big dog's feet with no place to go. He winks his eye at Vestal: "I suppose everyone around here knows that it takes a fellow like me, Big Damon as they say, to graft these papershell pecans."

Yes. Everybody calls him Big Damon and I call him Big Damon too. But he's my Grandpa just like Grandma's my Grandma. Reckon I couldn't say Grandpa to Big Damon if I wanted. 'Cause it's like putting him side by side with Grandma, and that ain't right even if they was married a long time ago.

"I tell you, Vestal, it's the way you graft the tree that makes the shell. Got to get a branch at just the right time. That's when the sap's running. And it ain't just any branch will do. Got to get a stout one from the Guadalupe River bottomland for these pecans if you want'em to be the grandkids of real kings."

"Papershell pecans," Vestal thinks some ageless water has washed them white while they hung on the weighted branches, even, crouching in green pods. She has watched them growing in Grandma's backyard on the old pecan tree Big Damon grafted before he left. Watched until her head got dizzy looking up the tree and down again to the grave at the base. And spinning around and around, she saw the first brown clusters hazy under the webs where spiders lived in the spring. Grandma would stop her watching: "There you, Vestal, you stop that gaping there like a li'l ninny." A miracle dream of spiders' webs and pecan papershells broken because her Grandma had to stop it: "Got to watch you all the time, young'un, or you'll be running on poor Ollie's grave. . . . My poor boy in that old wooden box, like we couldn't afford him a decent burying. . . . It was his idea of a-burying, and shameful I call it."

Big Damon's fingers snap, cracking pecans. He digs out little bronze sections of meat, tight-fitting in tan-fading-to-white shells. Two or three pecans fall on the floor, sap-filled marbles leaking through shriveling grandfather branches.

"The kernel ain't hard to find if you know just where to crack'em." Massive and gaunt-faced, Big Damon sits looking at the long naked core inside, grandchild of a rich river bottom, progenitor of a king-sized pecan. And while his sharp eyes inspect hard, his ancient nose sits still—that nose which came from his grandmother, the Comanche girl who married Lucien Callamades, a Spaniard-Frenchman.

Vestal is thinking: *and she . . . Mourning Water . . . was just fifteen and ran off from milking a cow to marry: and with no shoes on and a hole in her apron.* But Vestal is saying: "Big Damon, didn't you plant the tree in Grandma's backyard?" Cotton print panties squirming on the rug in front of Big Damon, Vestal almost remembers what she saw in a dream she once had about him.

"Yeah, and I grafted'em the spring you were born . . . and your mother, my own Vestie, held you there watching. You was a tiny babe. I never thought your mother would be gone so soon. She was a strong girl and happy, my Vestie, and it wasn't right to me, do you hear? I mean them a-praying over her and not getting a doctor. She died, my strong girl, and, well, Ollie lived on."

Ollie had it first and Mother caught it while tending him and Ollie got well and Mother died. I was just a baby. She was strong and Ollie was always weak, Grandma said, and she says too: "Sinful I call it, burying my poor Ollie later on under that pecan tree in a wooden box. It was his idea!"

Once Vestal dreamed Big Damon was a pecan, and watching his leather-yellow skin in the weak light of his lonely hotel room, she thinks she sees his skin fading into a cracking white shell. In the dream it was like a big pecan was cracking open and each crack was cutting though a current of time until the wrinkled kernel inside was laid naked for an instant, and Vestal peeped.

"What you been studying in school, Child?" Big Damon never talks long about the summer his daughter died. "Been making the grade in history; is it still your mark?"

And she was just fifteen and Callamades asked her to go when she was milking a cow. And they run off: her standing there marrying and holding a bouquet of bluebonnets like she sewed on the quilt—an Indian girl with no shoes on and a hole in her apron.

"Well, I been studying 'bout Bowie and Fannin and how they fought old Santy Anna at Goliad. You ever been there—to Goliad?"

"Yeah. . . . Goliad's a town near Cuero and Gonzales, not too far from where the Callamades first settled. . . . Hey, what you doing, Child, sitting on the floor?"

And before it was a republic, there was four nations ruling over Texas . . . the Indians they came first, then it was the Spaniards, the French, and then came the Mexicans.

Big Damon waves his arms at Vestal. He looks part ghost, she thinks.

I guess it's because he wears white overalls all the time and look at the black streaks on them. He gets 'em black painting houses, and they're brown and green streaks from painting brown and green roofs. He smells like a tree in resin time . . . and looking at him with those streaks is like that dream . . . only what was it like now . . . in that dream . . . once there inside?

"I said, what are you doing on the floor, Child? Don't you know a chair's for lay-dees, and say you won't be the first one to sit in my leather chair neither."

Cotton print-panties against flaking leather, she wishes she could move back to the floor and look at Big Damon's chair.

Grandma says don't sit in the seat of sinners. Says Jesus said so. Says it was sinful burying him under the tree and him so sweet and prayerful laying there in a little wooden box.

"There, that's better. A chair befits any lay-dee who comes visiting Big Damon. I'll swear if you ain't some squirmer, though. Just like my Vestie. . . . No, she never could stay still neither, always hopping around and laughing just like you. A strong girl too . . . and your Grandma always after her, her

32

and Ollie both with them praying sprees."

Named him Oliver but called him Ollie, Grandma says, because he wasn't strong from a baby on. . . . He'd stand around all quiet and praying and talking about eternal peace.

"So you're making it fine with your history, are you? Reckon you couldn't tell me what's the state flower?"

"Bluebonnets. My teacher says they grow all over hillsides, and I'm always seeing them on graves."

"That's true . . . say, let me tell you how they got their name. A long time ago the Indians was very sad. It was Comanche folks out on the plains that was all downcast. You see they'd been having lots of trouble. Couldn't grow no corn and berries because of a drought and they was a cold and hungry bunch. The chiefs and the medicine men called a council fire and asked the Great Spirit to help'em. And the Great Spirit told them that afore their suffering ended to make a burnt offering, something meaningful to the whole tribe.

"Now the chiefs and medicine men didn't know it, but while they was praying and invoking the Great Spirit the high chief's daughter was listening and taking in all they was saying. Now it happened too she was holding a li'l doll close to her heart. . . .

This li'lo doll was made of doeskin and had long black braids of horsehair, and on its head was a head-dress of bright blue feathers.

"Well, this little Indian princess told herself: 'I know the most precious possession of the tribe. I know what I got to do.' So when all the tribe was asleep she hugged her doll close and slipped out of the teepee where her father was sleeping. Her moccasins didn't make a sound as she was taking a red coal from them that had been the council fire but was now all covered with ashes. She went to a hill close by and built a little fire. On the fire she laid the precious doll, praying to the Great Spirit for her people to have food and happiness again.

"But all at once the wind caught up the ashes and scattered them all over the hillside. The little princess patted the ground where the fire had been to make sure they wasn't a spark left, and under her hands she felt something soft, but she couldn't pick it up on account of it was fastened to the ground. And next morning that whole hillside was a beautiful sight, for Child, do you know what? Why, that hillside was covered with bright blue flowers—just the color of the doll's head-dress.

"But this ain't all. There's more. When

the chief learned of what his li'l girl had done, he called all the Comanches together and told them: 'The Great Spirit has taken our offering and evil passed from us. These here blue flowers are sent us as a sign of peace and plenty.' "

And there's bluebonnets standing on Ollie's grave, waving in the wind and sometimes getting beat against the ground when the pecans fall down . . . it's sad . . . that grave.

Big Damon is his happiest when telling Vestal stories, but he loves talking to her about their region almost as much: "Can you tell me the bird for this state?"

"Sure. It's a mocking bird, that's what."

Once I heard one singing over Ollie's grave, first like one bird, then like another. Sitting there so bold and making a wild crazy chatter.

"Say, when I was a boy I used to whistle at them birds, and they'd always whistle back like they was laughing at me with their mocking. You know them birds is such experts at mimicking other sounds and birds, and keeps up such a constant repeating of whatever they chirp, both day and night, a boy can get an uneasy notion that they might be trying to tell him something about his future. Well, as a kid I used to wonder about that, but, of course, after I growed up I came to understand that they wasn't laughing at me at all; in fact that they didn't know anything much about life, except just how to make that aimless chatter as they tried to imitate us folks. . . . Anyhow, you're sure making your mark today. . . . Well, you told me what the state flower and bird is. Now what about the tree?"

"Miss Gammon says it's the pecan tree. She's my art teacher, and she has us make all kinds of things in class. She says the tree stands for friendship, so we ought to use it to make something for our friends. And so that's how come I made something for you, and here it is. I got an A in her class for doing it too."

Vestal hands her grandfather a pecan on which she has painted a gaunt face with an Indian nose. Two black eyes made of tiny black beads stare out from the shell while a sharp sliver of rock placed in the position of a nose sticks straight out over a body unbowed and imposing. On the gaunt face she has painted a gash to make lips, which are firm, wide, and relentless; a brow with a deep crease in it between the sharp eyes, and some marks to show hollow, sunken-in cheeks. A dot below the mouth also suggests a spare but uplifted chin.

Vestal has set the head on a cardboard cut-out body with painted white overalls.

There are black streaks running up and down the overalls, and brown and green ones too.

"Well, Lordy, if that don't beat all," Big Damon laughs. He lifts Vestal up, tosses her gently in the air, and then puts her down again. And all the time he rocks hard with laughter at this unexpected gift. Vestal titters too, pleased with his thankfulness.

They stop when the door springs open, and Grandma runs into the room, her minister behind her, but fixing himself conspicuously at the door. "You take your filthy hands off that child, you old devil," Grandma screams out running straight toward Big Damon, an umbrella thrust out at him as though it were a sword.

"Now Sister, let me handle this, please," pleads the minister as he rushes up behind her and takes her by the arm. "Kidnapping ain't nothing for a righteous God-fearing Christian like you to have to be a-coping with."

All this time Big Damon has just been standing there, the lines of his recent laughter and enjoyment with Vestal over her gift freezing now into the stony, impassive ridges his face becomes, his mouth forming the wide, harsh line which suggests mockery rather than pleasure. All he can do is watch

comtemptuously, yet with a sense of disbelief, as Grandma struggles loose from the
preacher. She comes over and shakes her
umbrella under Big Damon's sharply-
chiseled Indian nose.

"For a long time I been praying for your
soul," Grandma screams on. . . . "I been
praying your wickedness would end, and
you'd be ready to meet your Savior, and
here you been making mischief right on top
of my prayers. Thought you'd get away
with it, then, did you? Kidnapping this
child and bringing her here to your sinful
old hotel room. . . . But the Lord called me
tonight at prayer meeting and led me here."

"That is to say, Mr. Damon, sir," said
the minister again, thrusting himself between the two of them. "The Lord led
Deacon Cryer through the alley off Main
Street tonight, and the Deacon saw you
leading this innocent child. . . . " But Vestal
interrupts: "That's not so. . . . I wanted to
come here. . . . I begged him to bring me
over here, and I'll keep coming back."

"You, Vestal," scolds Grandma. "You
hush letting him put words in your mouth.
We know what he's up to and we won't let
him hurt you. He can't be trusted ever
again. He killed my Ollie . . . just as sure as
if he'd pushed him out of that tree."

At last Big Damon speaks, his words roaring out: "She lies. It's blasphemy, that's what. The kid was weak and sickly and after he got up from that bed of typhoid he went half-wild, praying all the time, just pushing my sick Vestie into her grave when what she needed was a doctor, not just a prayer, to keep her away from a coffin. And after she was gone . . . I couldn't help it. I lost my temper one day and started to whip him. I was doing it just so's I could straighten him out. But he ran off from me and climbed that tree. Poor confused little scamp of a guy! He did it, weak as he was, before I could get to him. I tell you that boy was losing his mind and it was all because of *your* continual Bible talking. He climbed up that tree I had just grafted and the limb broke under him."

"You drove him crazy telling him he killed Vestie, like he ought of died instead of her. But I knowed God had spared him to be a preacher," shouts Grandma.

Big Damon trembles. Standing up straight, he shakes his yellowed fists above Grandma's and the minister's heads. He cries: "Now get out of here. Out, damn you. Yeah, you can take the kid home with you. . . . I ain't saying it's any place for her to be here with an old coot like me. But don't start thinking I ain't going to see her ever . . . and what's more, just you satisfy yourselves that I'm not about to let you kill her either with your praying sprees and crazy palavering, the way you killed my Vestie. No sir, as long as she's a little girl, Big Damon will be around to keep an eye on Vestal here."

Grandma grabs Vestal by the hand, and as she starts toward the door screams again: "We'll run you outa town. . . . " And the minister pleads all the while: "Please folks. Let's stop this and have a word of prayer and then take the child home quietly."

But Big Damon reaches him in two angry steps, picks him up by the coat and pushes him through the door. "Ain't no praying and cavorting and jabbering a-going on under my roof."

As Vestal is dragged down the hallway past him, she can see one of his hands. And she knows she will never forget her glimpse of that little pecan doll, now cracked and torn inside his palm.

And looking, she remembers: *in that storm it was a tree, and its branches were shaking pecans off onto a little grave underneath. Then it thundered and one great pecan—a whitish-colored one which had black stripes—came crashing down and cracked open. It was just lying there cracked naked*

41

on the grave below.

And then it was so quiet in that place that the stillness seemed to take on life, to live with the blue flowers covering up the kernel . . . the seed . . . like an ancient quilt waving in the wind.

* * * * * *

The Sign from
Luke XVIII

Down a lane of sand and wind and scrubby grass, this grey house stands, and several who grew there, while the china berry tree grew old, do live there still; and some dwell there . . . away.

Who and for what and why?

They come to this place, and stay or leave it; yet all—even those who seem to barely pause in flight here to some place else—they too, like all the rest, become a part of it.

This morning Roddy, the baby girl (for they still call her that even though she passed her eighteenth birthday last July) is leaving this house. T.C. is on the door-stoop, scooping sand over his fingers in pyramids, and waiting to take his sister

away. All that's left of the family now—
Maudie, Vi, and T.C., of course, for he will
do the driving—are taking Roddy to college, in the little Chevy. T.C. bought it to
court Vi in six years ago; paid for it painting
houses. Somehow it seems older than that
now, this funny square-shaped thing with
its black canvas top, looking like a little two-
toned beetle, but sitting as if it is going to
topple off its high, round wheels any moment.

T.C. sizes it up: newly painted, green, always that color, and so shiny in the hot sun.
Many of his neighbors are riding in worse
outfits during these depression years. If the
radiator needs more water, he can always
put a little in. He goes to see.

Vi is at the window. She is watching T.C.
from inside the grey house which is his
mother's. Her eyes are following his swift
steps, going all the way up his long body to
his nervous hands and stringy ash-colored
hair, and following him with tension in the
frown on her face. Dashing outside, she
poses herself at the car, before him, with her
hands on her hips. "Looky here, T.C. I jes'
hope you've put enough gas'n water in that
buggy to get us home in time for Poppa's
barbecue tonight. You've forgot about
Poppa's birthday party now ain't'cha?"

The door of the house slams before T.C. can answer. Roddy runs outside and stops at the border of the rock-pile fence, which shelters the home place from the lane passing it. Roddy is a stocky girl for her tiny height, with hair that's too curly—short and blonde. Her skin is a salmon-color, splotched with brownish-red patches. She runs back and forth carrying canned goods from the door-stoop out to the fence, finally completing her trips when she sets a tired valise on the ground nearby—a cardboard carry-all of the kind that people in her part of the world usually keep hidden under beds and bring out only long enough to open, so that they can hide old letters, cheap books and newspaper clippings inside.

When Roddy comes outside, a warm dust folds itself around the three of them. It blows out of a world of sand and grass. T.C. takes no notice of her arrival, but then he is standing out in the driveway at a good distance off, busy with the car and intent upon watching the water he is pouring into the radiator from a long-nosed can. But Vi comes straight over to Roddy and says in a tone inaudible to T.C.: "Say, there's sumthin' I been meanin' to ask you when I could git you alone, but that never seems to happen no more!" And without giving

Roddy a minute to react, she leaps into her question, her eyes fixed on the girl: "You and Freddy . . . you two have had a quarrel now, ain't'cha?"

"Nothing between us to quarrel about," Roddy mumbles, eyes lowered, her body young and quivering in its effort to stand fixed to any given spot.

"You're sayin' you and Freddy are through, then?"

"I'm sayin' we never started. You know as well as I do that Freddy's . . . well, that he's a. . . . " " . . . a married man, you mean. Yeah, but I must say that his bein' married didn't seem to make much difference last summer. Why, the whole town was noticing how . . . ," but Vi stops abruptly when the door of the grey house opens and Maudie comes outside.

Maudie is wearing a pink dress, made of voil, flowery, and ornamented half way down the middle by a mother-of-pearl buckle. It holds the garment together in a bunch over something hard-looking underneath the thin material, clearly a corset, for its spine stands outlined in her snug-fitting skirt. Maudie has arms of soft, white fat, which even now remain unacquainted with the sun she has somehow managed to keep outside her dress-sleeves all her life. Her eyes are warm—brown-to-greenish pools, but they look worried in a face outlined with bedded, silver ringlets: "Now, honey, I declare, I bet you've went right off and forgot that pretty sign to hang up on your walls." She seems to voice her words in a somewhat distracted, half-scurrying way as she waves her hand toward Roddy: "Listen, child, you're *surely* gonna be wantin' somethin' to remind you of home up there at nights. . . . I've always said, and don't I know it's so, that it's always best to have sumthin' from your own place to look at in a strange room. . . . And it's a right pretty little sign too. A good reminder. . . . Says 'SUFFER LITTLE CHILDREN TO COME UNTO ME' in big letters, an' then in small ones: 'and forbid them not; for of such is the kingdom of heaven.' I know I've always found it comfortin' to look out of my bed way in the night and find them words from Luke Eighteen shinin' an' glowin' out to me through the dark from the wall of the bedroom."

"No, Mama, it's here; I put it in my suitcase. It's always been kinda special to me, ever since Pa brought it home from that carnival, 'n that happen'n like it did not so long before he died," Roddy says solemnly and with a voice which stands for once in concrete sureness.

They are all ready to go now. They climb into the high faded imitation-leather seats, and T.C. backs the Chevy into the lane.

Roddy looks out the dusty car window as they drive off and swallows, not really wanting to leave the grey house, which sits so shabbily on a dirty, sandy lane. It's a strange house with a stoop and rock-pile fence in front hunched next to a vacant lot of high brown-burned grass. Maudie's eyes are on her lap, puzzled: *"She's really leaving me now, this minute, but why does it happen so fast? How can you know all along that it's gonna be, and then have it come sneaking up on you all of a sudden, around a turn, just coming in so fast . . . happening, and you never knowing how it happened?"*

Roddy sees the other houses down the street. Today they rise up gaunt, seem so unaccustomed to the land; somehow they stand so silently, distantly from life, with no window curtains flapping to wave "so long." To her it is like the houses face her bland and embarrassed under the bane of hot heat; perhaps she once could see them as friendly only because she never really looked at them closely, but left them to stand forgotten among the accustomed.

Old Man Robinson sits on his porch, stiffly, eyes on the distance; yet no more than a part of his own porch. T.C. toots his horn; from inside, they wave—all of them—out the windows. Roddy leans outside to call: "'Bye, Uncle Harry," forgetting that he has been deaf all her life. His eyes, usually so alert for his ears, do not see them until he smells the dust the car makes passing, and he turns in his chair, his eyes wondering up the road: how did they pass without my seeing?

They pass Freedlove's house, dark with shutters drawn against the beginning afternoon, and dark through the rest of the day into the night. Somewhere inside they know there is Harrison Freedlove—the only son of the Methodist minister—slouched in his chair each day on his side of the house, and Avis Freedlove—bride of a forgotten romance—moving around on her side. An ancient dog growls and runs out from a dark retreat, snapping at the car-wheels, seeming to embody the spirit of his master.

"They say it's *him*—Harrison Freedlove—stirring up all those Methodists against us an' our sacred foot washin'," Maudie sneers. "He's always pokin' fun at whatever's meanin'ful, like our Fifth Sunday singin'. He's surely the biggest proselytizer in these parts," she charges further, referring to the long feud between the Methodists and the Primitive Baptists.

Leaning out of the back window, she addresses the gaunt Freedlove house: "Mister Freedlove, Sir! You jus' get bizy 'n call that dog. . . . " "Mama. Puleeze!" Roddy pulls her back inside the car. But it is not her mother that Roddy is looking at, it is at Freedlove's gate. For Roddy sees him first, standing there, Freddy Sears. He's just off the side of the road, leaning, supported by his right arm against a cottonwood tree. The shade of the tree is on his cool, dark face. And he looks straight inside, into the car.

They have arrived at the gate that opens onto the main highway, which by-passes their lonely town. Freedlove has this section of the gravel road, which is actually the short-cut from their house to the larger thoroughfare, fenced off so that he can remind people that the road goes through a section of his property, even though he tells people it's so that he can keep stray animals out of his garden, a place of high weeds and unattended for years.

T.C. must stop the car now, climb outside and open the gate. He does not look at, or say anything to, Freddy as he does so, and Freddy does not say anything to him. Freddy just stands there fixed in one motion, looking straight inside the car without so much as stretching his neck, but with a thin smile on his tight, hard lips. He spits a twig from the corner of his mouth as though he has been biting on it for a long, long time and is now tired of it. Mr. Freedlove's dog is still growling.

Vi stares at Freddy, then turns to look in the back seat at Roddy, whose eyes are on her lap. T.C. climbs back into the car, not saying a word, but slamming the car door hard against the ancient dog poised to run again with tired leaps at the wheels.

"Why, I never saw the like," murmurs Maudie in an annoyed tone, her eyes intently looking through the back window of the car, and focusing on the boy who is still standing there fixed to the same spot, his eyes almost harshly on their car. "Just WHO is is that boy? In my time a young buck wouldn't have dared not to open a gate for his neighbors."

"Eb Sears' boy, that's WHO. You know 'im, as well as I do," retorts T.C. He pushes the car ahead with a jerk, his foot hard on the accelerator, as they leap onto the highway. "An' what's more, I swear I ain't gonna stop again to close that damned thing. Ain't no sense it's being a gate there anyways with that danged 'ole dog always hangin' around to snap at the least little thing."

"What's that! You say it's Eb Sears' boy? Maudie starts in again.

"In the flesh," says Vi.

"Why, I thought he was that afflicted one. In a wheelchair these last ten years as I recall . . . ," Maudie continues with assurance.

"That's his brother. There never was nuthin' wrong with this 'uns legs," wagers Vi.

"You don't mean that this is the youngest one! I do declare he's grown. Say, I remember now. He was born just before Roddy came, and my look-it him now. You know I clean forgot about him. Say, I don't recollect seeing him a single Sunday at church since he was just a tot," Maudie remarks excitedly.

"I don't reckon you ever will either," says Vi.

"How's that?" Maudie asks, and in the next moment questions Roddy: "He ought to have been among your graduating class? Oh say . . . wasn't he the little boy that used to send you all those valentines when you was in grade school?"

"He quit school, Mama. . . . He was in the Tree Army . . . I mean the C.C.C.'s . . .

a long time," Roddy tells her mother in a weak voice.

"But he's come back now. My and how! Nearly runnin' that poor young wife of his nutty," Vi chimes in.

If she hears, Maudie registers no reaction; her attention is suddenly drawn entirely to Roddy's pale color: "Baby, you gettin' car sickness again? T.C., you know how she cain't ever get used to the back set of a car!"

"But, Mama," says Roddy quickly.

"Cain't you all move those canned goods into the back seat, T.C., and let her set up front with you? She jus' never was no good about ridin' in the back seat of a car since she was a baby," pleads Maudie.

"Maybe she oughta . . . ," begins Vi, again, eyeing Roddy sharply, and T.C. turns around in his seat, too, his eyes off the road and on the back seat: "Sure 'nuff. Say, Roddy, I'll just stop down the road apiece under that tree 'n you'n Vi kin git out 'n change places."

"Aw . . . it's aw . . . right," Roddy tells him.

Vi sits up front biting her bottom lip in silence, trying not to talk, but breaking out anyhow: "I can see how I should of stayed home again. Seems like I'm always in the way when I want to be with my husband," but she stops cold when T.C. looks at her. She turns from his gaze and finishes in a weak pout: "Always in the way, that's all."

"I know you like to be in the middle of things, Vi," Maudie blurts out, addressing her daughter-in-law directly in one of the rare times she ever calls her by name. "I well know you don't like to give up a front seat, but it's just that Roddy never could stand the back seat of any car." Then, Maudie adds, whimpering: "Son, it's like anytime your folks ask the least li'l favor of you, they're somehow in *her* way, thet's all. Now, lemme tell you, it's a mighty different matter any time it's *hers* on the askin' end!"

"Mama, Mama," pleads Roddy. "Say, Mama, listen! I'm all right, Mama, right where I am!"

"Jesus H. Christ! Do you all want me to stop this here car in the middle of the road? I can do thet, you know," threatens T.C., and warning: "A fellow gets pretty damned nervous drivin' in this traffic on the hottest pavement in Texas, or on this side of billy hell for that matter."

There is a long silence before he adds: "An' a-course Roddy's gonna ride in the front seat with me, 'n thet's all there is to it, 'n it ain't gonna make a Sam Hill of differ-

ence to nobody."

There is not a car in sight of them on the silent road which oozes ahead in the sun-soft pavement, the bumps filled with tar squashing underneath the tires. Spinning around and around, T.C.'s wrist jerks angrily at the wheel. Outside the land floats by swimming in the vapor of the dead September air. The flat brown-to-grey dead earth of burned grass rolls on and on like an empty graveyard among the monotony of turns and curves in this highway, which a crazy man seems to have engineered in a pattern of zig-zags through a treeless waste. Now and then a tiny mound of ground rises in the highway or a cattleguard cuts an abyss in the tired and sluggish earth. That is the only change. They say they cut the highway where the trees wouldn't grow. The houses in front of the tiny corrals, and the barns to the sides glare forward and shrink backward in a kind of macabre rhythm with the motor of the car in the haze so real that the violent blue sky yields down that it makes the land look surreal. Only one half-cloud drifting in from the Gulf of Mexico dizzily casts its shadow in the distance, keeping aloof, though; belonging really to the seashore that lies a couple hundred miles away to the south.

In the silence of T.C.'s command, they bear silence each to each, and watch instead, inside this jumbled, stifled mass of reality, the reality that comes from considering the earth, in knowing that heat like this has driven men crazy. Each of them is apart, but fear is riding the frantic air between. Each is knowing now that something is starting; that something must, will start any minute.

It starts at once with Roddy.

"Oh, dear God," she wails, pleading as the sickness wells up and heaves over into its nasty mass. It comes boiling out as glassy tears spew forward from her staring, blue eyes. "Oh, the dear Lord God." From the back seat, Roddy is suffered against the front, tossed around by her own tumult and shouting, fighting at each retch that comes shaking out of her small stocky body. "Oh, help me! Do come help me," she begs in terror. But the sickness rolls on and over in monotony with this land they journey through, and mounts again and again to tear and reap before T.C. can stop the car. Roddy grabs at the front seat, but it sways away from her. Around her, the family sits in silent horror, in disbelief; they seem to shrink away from her; maybe in hatred of themselves; perhaps in revulsion at their own bodies. They seem to go inside themselves and feel their own weak flesh riding along too with hers in this furious, violation they have been forced to witness.

The car has stopped at the first gas station to be found, but the sickness has already subsided. T.C. gets out to wet his handkerchief at the water cooler for his sister. Roddy lies lost in the back seat, still in a semi-convulsed state from the last spasms of her illness, her pulse still racing. Her head is now sheltered in her mother's lap, and Maudie is above it, murmuring softly: "My poor baby!"

Roddy lies there, coming back to find her former self, coming back with a little streak of cool wind, which somehow manages to stray through the car from under the shadow of the filling station's runway. She feels the trickle of the cold, clean drops of water springing down her forehead from the wet handkerchief T.C. has thoroughly saturated for her under the water cooler. She thinks of how the water on her skin is like drinking the well water from the dipper that hangs over the bucket of water on the back porch at home, and about how the feel of it is also like that of getting into cool sheets at night. She remembers how good it is to come away from the hot chairs of daytime and go into the cool sheets of night at home, nestled in her own bed.

Now she begins to feel the first coursing of strength through her blood, an initial creeping of power, a newborn vigor. Its essence seems to impart to her that she has peeped inside the core of pain and looked past her suffering to a certain undeniable beauty. And though she knows she will avoid remembering her agony, she knows still that she can never forget glimpsing its nameless and dreadful face. For she realizes that despite her loathing of remembering all that is a part of her new awakening, she feels a curious pride in knowing it. She is aware that in its very abuse, somehow, her suffering has cleansed her, has brought her this mounting of fresh power in the very sinews of her flesh.

Or is this what it is? Maybe she can never say that it is this or that. Perhaps she can only say that she has experienced a truth for the first time, and with the security which comes in seeing and knowing it she is no longer afraid.

Roddy feels loneliness in this truth.

Maybe she would give up all this new power, give it back, all the knowing of it, to be simply as she was before it came.

Roddy feels the lap of her mother where

her head now rests. She feels the hardness of
the corset against her face, and her mother's
breathing, too, against the corset. And she
knows that under the corset, holding like a
prison her mother's lap, the flesh is very
soft. She remembers knowing its welcome
warmth when as a little girl she used to bury
her head in her mother's lap just to feel the
soft, warm stomach rise and fall under a
thin cotton dress. She thinks that she is
lonely now because somehow it all seems
that things have switched and she is wearing the corset now; that because she is wearing it, she has found out that it can be used
to shield herself from almost any pain.

Vi bends over her. An awkward look is on
Vi's face, but it is an unmistakably kind one
with gentle worry lines. Vi reaches one
hand slowly toward Roddy, almost touching her sister-in-law; but she lets it fall back
to her side. Instead she says in blurted, busy
words, the lines on her brow wavering between harsh and gentle ridges: "Here, you
take it, Roddy . . . well, why'n the world
don't you just go ahead and take it!"

Roddy blinks hard. Vi is standing over
her, and she is dressed in one of Roddy's old
skirts, one which isn't even ironed. It raises
way above Vi's knees too. Also Vi has on
Roddy's oldest blouse. "I *do* want you to

take it," Vi insists rather timidly.

It is Vi's new cotton blue dress that is being offered. Roddy can smell it as she touches it: still starched and fresh-to-sweet, in this day's wear in the hot sun. It is like everything Vi wears is always bathed in cool perfume, like her name: Violet June.

"It's sweet of you, but I just couldn't, Vi. Why, it is your new dress, and it took you days to make it. No, I wouldn't think of takin' something like that away from you," Roddy protests.

"Aw, Roddy, you go'n ahead an' take it. Don't I want jus' that? Ain't that why I changed clothes and brought it over here to you? Besides ... I still got two or three yards of material, all new, at home. It's that stuff Sister brought me from the sewing room when we thought.... Well, you know, when I lost that baby. I still got to make it up, and ... well, you cain't never tell," she continues proudly, the stark barren truth of five years behind the wanting to believe *it isn't true* glistening in her eyes. "Why, y'all don't know ... one of these days I'm jus' liable to have a real surprise for everybody."

The viper heat is breaking now with the beginning of sundown. Beads of sweat spot

Roddy's brow as the Chevy moves into the first round green turn of the town of San Marcos. There are quiet cool houses here where the fans have been going all afternoon. The hot adobe and the stuccoed houses stand in the dampness of their spent, tired plasters; they rest in the shade of trees.

The college rises on the one hill called Pilot's Point. The college is really just one dormitory and an administration building with a silver dome. Roddy knows from what her favorite teacher once told her that there is a light which shines from this dome while the students at this girls' school sleep. She remembers how her teacher said that some of the students, when waking between midnight and dawn, have seen the light make a cross, its rays extending down the hill into the valley that is the town.

Roddy is watching the hill move closer and closer into view, as they ride toward it up the Main Street of San Marcos. In Vi's cool dress, the early evening wind soothing her hair, her face flushed excitedly, her hands trembling so that she can not hold them still, Roddy is feeling her spirit approach this hill. To herself she is saying: "Pa always wanted me to go up there. He said I was born to be a teacher."

"My, looky," whispers Maudie, in half as

much belief as disbelief, as the college rises closer and closer on the hill. "My, oh my! Don't I wish I was this young'un."

Up the hill on all sides, everywhere, driving, walking, or stopping to talk are girls, or girls and their parents. Sometimes a boy or two is among them, but always looking out of place. Mostly just more girls is all that one can see.

"Would you all just see that," Vi points to a group of the youngest-looking girls around. They wear jaunty, blue caps perched at cocked angles on their heads. The face of each is disfigured with lipstick streaks and symbols painted in rouge.

"It's because they're newcomers; that's why they are gettin' initiated," T.C. proudly informs his listeners. "Golly, wouldn't any li'lo banty rooster have himself a time here! Woowee! Yes siree!" And before any of the women can interrupt to scold, he sniggers: "Ain't that big old fat gal with the bonnet on her head a regular sight for sore eyes!" Then he and his female audience laugh wildly as they hunch forward and stare out the side-windows of the automobile, all of them intently absorbed in witnessing the fat girl doing a war dance. She is comically lifting her arms and waving them around in mid-air, and what is more grotesque, attempting to hold still, somehow, her shaking, blubbery hips by no less a trick than taking certain rigid, stiff steps. The older girls form a circle around her, yelling taunts of laughter and whoops over their shoulders to the group of younger girls standing huddled together, apart from them.

"Fatty sure don't mind the laughs, does she? You'd think as big as she is, she'd dig herself a cellar and stuff herself up in it 'til she gets her degree. I know I sure would if I was as big 'n ugly as she is," Vi observes, calculating the every movent of the obese freshman.

Maudie cautions Roddy: "Never can tell what they'll make you do, honey. But now jus' so's you don't let them make a fool out of you, it's all right. Why, you just get in there 'n show'em what a fine spirit you've got." In a dry whisper, she adds quickly: "You jus' remember too, honey, that you're jus' as much a lady as the fanciest one of them. You do that for my sake. Hear that, Roddy?"

They do not hear her when it begins, for they are watching so intently, contemplating so completely this new land of Roddy's, daring to peek hard at it, to stare openly, to remember all they can of this unusual place.

Seeing it in admiration, they are ashamed to look at each other, for each is ashamed to find the betrayal of his own reverence in the other's eyes. So they cling silently, but inadequately and timidly together, jealously guarding their fierce pride, worth more to them than any answer is, even the simplest one. They will diligently search and search alone to find that answer in the silence of their own individual awakenings. It is their way. A way they have been taught without words by their ancestors: this idea of theirs that they must ever sense or only question silently what is really new to them; that they must talk endlessly about the little things and never ask openly for the answers to the big things, the things to which they are unaccustomed.

So they do not hear her cry at first, for each of them is engrossed in his own way with questions to answer about this new land. They do not hear at first. Then, it breaks through to them that Roddy is crying into the crumpled handkerchief that T.C. gave her earlier that afternoon, and fighting to drown her sound, for only short muffled noises escape. When she sees they are noticing, Roddy is overcome with shame. Her words rush out behind bitter tears: "Papa said I was born to be a teacher."

Maudie touches her daughter, bewildered by her grief, talking softly to her all the while: "Child, child! Goodness knows if you aim to be a teacher, then there sure ain't nuthin' here . . . jus' nuthin' . . . that can ever stop you, can it? Why this is the very place to come to for such a goal, ain't it? Land knows you're just about to get started, ain't you? So come on, now, and be happy. You've got the best kinda chance to do well. Why, I'd give my last shoes just to be standing in yours."

Despite her mother's efforts to calm her, Roddy wails on: "He said I was just born to be one."

"An' who's sayin' he's wrong about that? I sure ain't. Why, you kin do anything you want. Don't let comin' to this place scare you, honey. You'll get on. Just look-it how you up an' got Dr. Norris' wife to sign all those papers for you, so's you could come up here in the first place. An' don't you up'n tell me that jus' any of these snippy li'lo girls I see around here that's had everything given to 'em would know how to land a scholarship. No siree! I know better. So, honey, don't you go worryin' about gettin' to be a li'lo teacher among a crowd like this. Honey, that's the silliest thing ever; for somebody like you, it's bound to be a snap. And don't 'cha start feelin' lonesome neither. Jus' think of all the frens you'll make up here an' how proud all of us that hasn't never had your chance are gonna be to git to come up here 'n see you. Now we'll come up often; jus' real often. Won't we, T.C.?"

"Sure, Ma. We'll come up so often I'll bet Roddy'll start throwing us out," assures T.C. He reaches back to pat his sister on the head, touching her a little awkwardly, ashamed over the need for such a display. "Everything's gonna be okay, Roddy."

"You oughtn't to cry, Roddy," says Vi. "Even if you are . . . well, you jus' oughtn'ta cry when I wish so hard. . . . " Roddy starts to calm down. With a grimace, she purses her lips and swallows her last tears. She sits rigidly, her fists clenched. A slight slump is in her body as she gives way to acceptance of her new role. "I'm sorry, you all. I guess I'm really aw'right now."

"Sure you're okay, Roddy. You're just feelin' a little homesick, honey. That's all it is, but that will pass," Maudie offers with assurance.

T.C. stops the car in front of the dormitory. A long chain of girls moves inside and outside the large, three-story building. They move in confusion—excited in their chatter, but betrayed by their nervous giggles. They seem to be forever picking up and setting down suitcases, or waving hellos and good-byes. Roddy turns her eyes away from them as she gets out of the car.

"Ma, I don't feel we should get out. It's so late and all. I'll jus' put her suitcases out-side. Then, I think we oughta leave. Maybe it's better this way . . . anyhow, the first time," suggests T.C. earnestly.

"But I wanted to help some with her room," begs Maudie.

"No, Mama, T.C.'s right. I'd rather you didn't," Roddy urges. She's standing on the outside, leaning back inside the car to touch her mother's hand.

"Ma, we've gotta be gettin' back. I prom-ised Vi," T.C. pronounces sentence firmly. "An' we're all tired out. Jus' how in the world would we look anyhow a-goin' in there all messed up in our clothes, an' espe-cially amongst all those fine folks?" He sets Roddy's suitcases on the curb outside the car.

"It *is* awful late, an' you know it took us a real long time to get here. We sure won't be makin' it out to my Dad's either," Vi re-sponds in a disappointed tone.

"Well, honey, you know how I'd like to

. . . , an' if it was just me, I'd most assuredly find a way, but if you'd really 'n truly rather . . . ," Maudie asks Roddy.

"Yes, Mama, please, I'd really rather you'd go straight on home," Roddy answers, her hand softly stroking her mother's.

"You'll write us every day, won't you, honey? Be sure 'n drop us a line about all your doin's, about all these nice girls, 'n about how you'n the teachers are gettin' on. Jus' put down every bit of it," Maudie insists to her youngest in a final plea.

"Yes, I'll write," she promises reaching in the car to kiss her mother good-bye and to get away before Maudie can hold her fast.

Everything begins to blur for her in the absurd haste in which the actual departure at last occurs; in the snatched kisses, pats on the hand, handclasps, and finally in the Chevy churning loudly into motion from its idle position. Suddenly she is alone in a wild, weird orbit of whirling loneliness. It rushes in and surrounds her as the car careens slowly out of the dormitory drive, and its occupants wave back for the last time as they pull out onto the highway. As she stands alone watching the car become two dots of dim tail lights on the road, she can still hear her mother's muffled crying. When she tries to move, she finds she cannot. Paralyzed in fear, she cannot leave this spot where they have brought her: the spot that they—whom she loves most—have touched. She cannot leave for a long time. When she does begin to walk away, it is as if she is in a daze. She does not even know that she is walking. She just picks up her suitcases and begins to follow another girl, who is walking toward the dormitory. She moves along behind the other girl as if a dream is commanding her to make the girl her leader. She can see the long, lighted hallway of the dormitory ahead; its rays of light on the sidewalk seem to be beckoning, almost welcoming her inside. She realizes she wants to rush ahead; she needs to enter and find warmth, for suddenly she is very cold. It seems to her as though every warm thing on earth lies waiting inside that door.

But she stops a little distance from the entrance. She drops her hands from her suitcases and stands frozen still. Her heart pounds loudly, and she is aware that her whole body trembles as she swallows up her last tears. Quickly she turns away, picks up her suitcases, and flies down the path back to the dormitory parking lot.

"Hello there. You look like you've got

some kind of trouble," an older girl calls out sympathetically to her as Roddy rushes past her down the path. But Roddy does not stop—not even for a second; she just keeps running. "Sure that I can't help you?" the girl calls out again. But Roddy does not seem to hear her; she only pushes ahead, mumbling disconcertedly: "What if *she* isn't waiting. Just what?" Over and over she whispers it hoarsely and frantically to herself: "What'll I do if she forgot an' left me up here!" It's night now. She runs on, looking in vain in the dark from car to car parked in front of the dormitory, peering sometimes among young lovers who are saying their farewells, or into the midst of other families involved in telling their daughters good-bye.

In the last car parked at the end of the lot, she finally locates Dr. Norris' wife, seated behind the steering wheel and talking in a low voice to another girl sitting beside her on the seat. Roddy comes up to the car door before they notice her.

When she sees Roddy, Mrs. Norris nods impatiently to her. "At last! We had just about given up on you. We've waited and waited. Been here at least an hour, if not two, and I was just saying to Madeline, here, that we ought to go on without you.

But we hated to. I want so much to get out to my daughter's tonight before she puts the baby to bed. You know I have a grandson living in San Antonio?"

"I'm sure sorry," says Roddy in a tired, timid voice. "I tried to make it as fast as I could, but things just seemed to keep blocking me," she apologizes further as she sinks wearily into the place they make for her on the front seat.

"Of course, I could just go right over to Madeline's house and pick her up. But not yours; that was a different case. Meet Madeline Chernofsky, Roddy. You two will probably be good friends over there in San Antonio."

Madeline does not respond. She does not look at Roddy. She has not looked at her since Roddy got inside the car, nor did she look at Roddy before. Madeline just looks straight ahead of her, a hard, dazed smile on her chalky, heavily mascaraed face. Accented in rouge, it looks like it has been stolen from a cast-off baby doll and glued to her neck to replace her real countenance.

"I was telling Madeline," continues Mrs. Norris, as she backs out of the dormitory lot and heads out into the long highway that stretches out before them in the direction of San Antonio; "this man says you can go to work tomorrow. Madeline knows him well. She was there before. He's employed several of our girls before to do odd jobs at his place, and kept them almost up to the very end. I think you surely ought to be able to work most of the time. Don't you think so? We want our girls to work as long as possible. You know when there's a depression on, money's hard to. . . . " Roddy sits in silence beside Madeline. She cannot answer. She cannot think of anything except the way she has watched the motion of Madeline's hand over the burden of Madeline's swollen stomach. Roddy is looking straight ahead of her, staring, straining to find the hill, where in the mist the light can take the shape of a cross. She is struggling to ignore the dense black highway ahead. Her lips are moving over and over, and she is repeating slowly, but really only to herself: "But Poppa said I was born to be a teacher . . . a teacher."

When Mrs. Norris finally makes out what Roddy is actually saying, she tells her softly: "Maybe if you can somehow manage to keep your child, it will be the same thing, honey. Like being a teacher, I mean."

Roddy thinks she knows all that Mrs. Norris is trying to say: for in her mind, she turns something over and over again to herself. It is the wording on that sign from Luke XVIII. Somehov that she is going to b the grey house where used to hang; standin the china berry tree o

* * *

*Once Again on
All Souls'*

Once again on All Souls', they took the food and roses from Tucson down to Sasabe, and put them on Buck's mother's grave at the candlelight service. Buck had been born in this little town in Sonora on the Mexican border. He always told Lillie that he believed his mother truly returned to earth there on that night and could see the candles and roses—usually artificial ones—he placed on her grave. Yes, and enjoy the food. He would always take her a plate of something tasty: generally, these days, a giant cheeseburger from "Whataburger" and a king-sized cup of coffee. Even though Lillie was a Baptist, she loved attending this ceremony with Buck.

In fact, she often told him that she looked forward to it each year as one of the nicest and most unusual things that she—Lillie Perry, a *gringa* from Texas—had done during her whole life.

Still she was always afraid she might see a rattlesnake as they kept their vigil by the grave. Though the snakes were plentiful in the area, Buck always teased her: "Now, Lillie, even over there in Texas, I bet they don't come out very often at night during early November." He would then laugh and slap Lillie on the thigh, whisper to her that the only snake he was going to let her see lots of anyway, night or day, was the snake he had tattooed on his wrist when he was a Pvt. in the U.S. Army Cavalry. At the same time, he would wiggle his wrist back and forth in front of himself until they both giggled wildly.

When Buck saw any friends from his youth at the annual vigil, and they asked how things were going, he would put his arm around Lillie, and say: "Oh, we're permanently located on 'the other side,' still up in Tucson, and still playing it the safe way." Then he'd take Lillie by the arm and walk away. Lillie always laughed when he told friends that. Buck knew that only she realized that, among other things, he meant

that they still lived in a Safeway parking lot
in Tucson in the 1970 GMC camper they
had driven down to Sasabe. Buck could see
she understood too that while he had been
christened Johnny Lopez in Sasabe, he now
preferred the name of Buck and was especially proud of his U.S. citizenship.

All evening he and Lillie would stay beside his mother's grave and drink from the
Gallo wine jug Buck had brought along. But
at midnight, they, like everyone else who
came to keep the vigil, would feast at the
grave on the same kind of lunch they had
brought his mother. After midnight when
all the visitors left the cemetery, they would
blow out the candles with which they had
neatly lined his mother's grave and go back
to the camper. Buck always parked it in a
secluded place. Once inside it, they would
promptly begin their own feast of all night
sex interrupted only by their continuous
drinking from another jug of Gallo. Their
ritual usually ended around dawn when
Buck often passed out. Such feats of endur-
ance were not uncommon to them, for even
though Buck was 65, and Lillie, 58, he never
let up on their sex life: a once or twice a
night affair, and on weekends even during
the afternoons. Lillie and it were all he lived
for. Besides he feared constantly that Lillie

would leave him if he didn't keep her satisfied. Still, they always made a special occasion out of All Souls' Night in Sasabe. At dawn, they would sleep a few drunken hours, and then in the afternoon they would slowly drive back to Tucson to a Safeway parking lot.

This time they drove to the Safeway at the corner of Grant and Alvernon. For the past six months they had spent every night here while the construction of a shopping mall went on around them. Buck and Lillie had been living together at Safeways over the state—Tucson, Phoenix, Mesa, Willcox, Benson—for four years now. But they preferred a Tucson location because the weather seldom made life in Buck's camper, really just a truck with a shell over its bed, unbearable. Also because they could visit often with Buck's son Timiteo and his family, and increasingly, too, with some of Buck's other children, who had now left home and worked at jobs of their own.

Buck knew that Lillie had had many men throughout her life; how many worried him. And she would never say. Of course, he knew she had been married at least three times, but that was okay with him. He had lived through a marriage and several relationships, all loveless, even though the marriage had been blessed by a priest. Since he was still not out of his marriage, either legally or in the eyes of the church, and Lillie knew it, he could not afford to complain about Lillie's husband. Despite their current situation, marriage was the subject Buck spent most of his time talking about, and desiring for them. But he knew Lillie didn't necessarily feel the same. In the early days when he first met her, he had been very unhappy because he had to share her with two other men—one a shoe salesman who met her at the bar where she had been a waitress, and the other her boss, who frequently took her to a back room while she was still on the job. Sometimes, even when Buck was drinking there and waiting for her. When Buck complained, she told him it was all just part of her job, adding: "Anyhow, you've got a wife the same as they do. You don't take care of me."

During those days, Buck was still officially living with his wife, Rosita, in a run-down trailer park in South Tucson, and the youngest of their eight children was just a tot. Also his older children were still dependent upon him. It was in those first years of knowing Lillie and being separated from living with her night and day that Buck nearly went crazy, for wherever he was, he thought of her constantly. When Buck knew Lillie was with some other man, he would quit his work, no matter where he was, go home and take Rosita over and over until she screamed. Sometimes he would pick up another woman just for spite. But no matter who was with him, Lillie was always in Buck's mind. Everywhere, all the time. He could never get enough of her. Now after four years of living with her under the camper shell, he knew he never would. But he could never be certain of the thing he wanted most—that Lillie would be his forever.

Buck had not been able to coax Lillie into living with him until he was able to buy the used camper on what was actually his sixty-first birthday. At that time, he was able to go on social security because his Army records were off one year. Though Buck had really come to the U.S.A. from Sasabe as a wetback, he had earned his new citizenship legally by enlisting in the cavalry in W.W.II. Even though he had entered the Army when he was seventeen (he needed a job to support his bride, Rosita), his records showed his Army service as beginning with his eighteenth birthday. When Lillie agreed to move into the camper with him, Buck had left the nagging Rosita in the trailer park with their children. By that time, though, Timiteo, the oldest, was already married; Johnny, Jr., the next, had joined the Navy; and the others were becoming less dependent daily.

Buck's sixty-first birthday had marked what had been the happiest day of his life. It was so because of his own choosing he had taken what he felt to be marriage vows with Lillie. On that day when she came to live with him in the camper, he had put upon her finger the gold ring, a keepsake from his mother. He had never given it to Rosita, whom he had been forced to marry in Mexico late in her pregnancy with Timiteo. With all his heart, Buck wished that Lillie had not passed the time to beget him children when he found her. But no matter. No younger woman would ever take her place. After Lillie came to live with him in the camper, Buck begged her almost daily to marry him legally, for he promised her he would find a way to divorce Rosita even if the Catholic church might not recognize it. But Lillie would only look off in the distance and tell Buck that she was still legally married to Laynie D. Kendricks back in her home town in Texas. She would also remind Buck that since he would always be a Catholic at heart, he too was more than just legally married to Rosita. During the day, when they found cast-off newspapers in the parks, Lillie would read them—especially the religious news—to Buck. His ability to read English never had been good. When Buck heard of any annulment given by the Catholic Church he would say: "Look here, Lillie. *Mira, cariño.* Let's you and me get hitched too. Now, Lillie, we could even go before the priest like those two have and say the words. You don't care nothing about that old guy Laynie, do you?"

"Now, Buck, stop that. You ain't got a legal divorce from Rosita, and besides, they wouldn't give you no annulment after eight children by her, and all of them inside marriage." Then laughing and punching him, she would add: "And no telling how many kiddos too on the outside? Eh? Besides, Buck, honey, I'm just as firm a Baptist as you are a Catholic, and we believe that once in grace, always in grace. No, Buck, I ain't planning on becoming a Catholic, even if I do like this All Souls' business."

At such times, Buck would pull the gold ring on Lillie's wedding finger over to his tattoo and say: "Ah, *cariño*, this makes us more husband and wife than any priest or preacher, no?" But Lillie would only laugh in a self-conscious way.

The truth was that even during the first year of their life together, Buck had been forced to allow Lillie to continue her relationship with Hugh Owens, the Phoenix shoe salesman, who traveled for Stylesaver's. In that year Buck had tried to do yard work from time to time so that they would have extra money. But often when he left Lillie alone in the camper, regardless of what parking lot or city they were living in, he might come back to find that Owens either was, or had been, with Lillie. The first time that he had discovered them together, he had tried to fight Owens, but Lillie had stopped him. "Just don't give me any static about it. Okay, fellows?" In fact, to the amazement of Owens, who was trying to ignore Buck, and Buck too, who was red with rage, Lillie had said calmly: "You guys had just as well shake hands as to beat up on each other, because you got to remember I'm the gal who decides what she wants and when." Afterwards Buck had learned not to mention it when he felt she had been with Owens, for he knew Lillie didn't see Owens only for some spare money; he knew she did it out of need. It was then Buck decided he had better quit leaving her during the day to go mow lawns. No, no matter how much they could use the money. It was then, too, that he began to drive them all over the state and to park in out-of-the-way Safeway lots and never near a Stylesaver's store. In this way he had finally succeeded in either losing Owens entirely or in confusing Lillie enough for her not to be able to tell him exactly where to meet her. Thus Buck's first year with Lillie was just a blur in his memory of long sexual feasting, mingled with relentless driving from place to place. It was expensive in gas, but at that time they still had food stamps, so Buck told himself it was the only way to solve the problem and avoid any further painful encounters with Owens.

During the past year of their life together, Buck had kept Lillie exclusively to himself. He felt some measure of success in the fact that he had also been able for six months now to keep the camper steadily on the parking lot in Tucson. Frequent night shoppers who caught sight of Lillie and him thought he was either a night watchman for the new Arizona Regional Savings Bank under construction, or else a daytime workman employed there. Looking towards them, some would even say: "You know it's a good idea to have a watchman like that around what with so many burglaries happening."

If they were close by, Buck and Lillie

would sometimes nod back, though Buck tried to keep as much distance from people as possible. Of course, he had never earned his living in such a capacity. After his discharge from the Army, he had always worked around rodeo pens, usually around Tucson, Willcox, or Benson. At first he had been a bronc-buster, earning early his name Buck, for it was true he could stay in the saddle with almost any bucking horse he met. Then he had worked at the loading chutes and last as a clean-up man around the arena and pens. It was only after he met Lillie that he had turned to the yard work. In one way, he had given up the horses in exchange for Lillie. For, from the night he met her, and succeeded right off in sleeping with her, he had lost interest in his frequent out-of-town work with horses.

This had been Buck's happiest year with Lillie. Watching her, he told himself it must be the same for her. Lillie had grown up in a small town called South Banks, where she had spent most Saturday afternoons, like her neighbors and friends, sitting in a car and watching the happenings along the main street. To Lillie, living on the parking lot was something like perpetually living out a Saturday afternoon at the center of things in South Banks. Yes, she loved being a part of the main hub. Her eyes always lit up when they hit the center at a rush hour. "Sure great to see business good, eh, Buck?" she would say, absorbed in the people and their cars as if she had a vested interest in them.

But, despite his happiness, Buck worried about the future. What would happen when Lillie could draw her social security pension like he did? Since she now had practically no money of her own (she kept just a few dollars in a little purse concealed in the camper in the pocket of an old sweater), she was completely dependent upon Buck and his pension. By living in the camper shell, they were just able to get by. Now that they weren't wasting their money on gas, they could spend more on food. Since they could not stand up very well in the camper, and since Lillie had always liked to eat out, Buck saw to it that she had to do as little cooking as possible. They ate their breakfast of donuts and coffee close by at the Bosa Donut House, and on weekends at Macdonald's. Their lunch was the daily special at Carrows, or at Jack-in-the-Box; sometimes a hamburger at Whataburger. For supper they bought canned goods from Safeway: pork and beans, sardines, or peanut butter. They ate on paper plates in some city park, where there were good tables and benches. Once a week, they got high on a big bottle of Gallo, though Buck always watched Lillie carefully if they were in some place where she might meet some new men when they were drinking.

Every night about seven they pulled up onto the Safeway parking lot, and every morning around seven, they left it for the day in Randolph, Ft. Lowell, or Tucson Mountain Park. If they learned of a flea market or a gala opening at some new shopping center, they would always attend it, enjoying the free samples and attractions, with Lillie hunting endlessly for the new sheets, towels, or necessities they needed for the camper or themselves.

Buck took great pains every night to park their camper in its usual spot. Sometimes he and Lillie would have to stay up until 11 or 12 p.m. just to get that spot. Buck was always upset if someone had beat them to it when they arrived. "Crazy bastards," he would grumble to Lillie if such were the case. "Damned fool kids got nothing better to do than hang around all night."

There was a Pizza Inn just around the corner from their space, and sometimes teenagers who gathered there for an evening of beer and talk would park one of their loud-motored hot rods in their space. At such times, Buck would spend most of the evening walking from whatever temporary spot he and Lillie had selected back and forth to the viewing window of the Pizza Inn. He would peer through it, and hope by some magic the offender would recognize the mistake that had been made, and then leave at once with the unwelcome vehicle. More and more frequently they found the spot vacant; it was as if the frequenters of the lot had come at last to realize that it should be reserved for them.

Their parking space was the most level spot on the whole lot. From it they could watch the sunset over the Tucson Mountains and the sunrise over the Rincons. They could usually depend on settling into their nightly routines around nine. If they had visitors coming they always parked in a different spot on the lot until they had finished visiting with them outside the camper. Buck felt this drew them and their permanent place less attention. After the company left, Lillie would always stay outside the truck and walk over to their spot so that she could direct Buck into the most level position in their space. She could not stand for the car to be anything but perfectly level. When the car was the slightest bit out-of-line, she would raise a ruckus that might last all night. This, of course, interrupted their sex life and everything else that surrounded the peaceful domesticity that at last seemed to be developing. Since Lillie asked so little else of him, Buck did his best to please her in this regard. Still he noticed that more and more people watched as Lillie motioned for him to back up just an inch or so more to the right, and a fraction less to the left. He was afraid someone was going to notify the police, who could consider them vagrants and penalize them in some way. But he was careful not to mention his concern to Lillie lest she suggest they start driving around again.

Since she had not confronted him with the threat of Owens for a long time now, he felt she must really like this spot too. Not that Buck still didn't keep a sharp eye out for Owens. There were several vacant stores for lease in the new mall, and from time to time when he was away from Lillie on an errand, he would stop some clerk he saw working at Safeway or Revco, and ask them: "Got any shoe stores coming in here? Any Stylesaver's?" He would point to the vacant buildings near the Yellow Front. If the clerk said: "I don't know, sir," Buck was satisfied. If, as was sometimes the case, they took his question to be the expression of a need for such a store, and said: "Yeah, we could sure use a good shoe store out here, couldn't we? You might go over to the cashier's box and talk to the manager about . . . ," Buck would worry for days.

These days Buck was getting to see much more of his children too. Timiteo and his wife, Margarita, especially carried messages back and forth to Buck from the youngest two, who were still living with Rosita. They even brought one or two of the older ones who were now working in Phoenix over to visit whenever they were in town. Buck delighted in watching Lillie with his family. This had been their first real opportunity to get to know her well, and they enjoyed being with Lillie and him so much that they were nightly visitors almost, especially Timiteo and his family. Since Lillie liked being around people, Buck felt that visiting his children was the best way to keep her occupied. So, at first, he encouraged them and his grandchildren to come over as much as possible. Otherwise Lillie might get bored, and he might have to take her to some bar.

More and more as she came to know Buck's children, Lillie talked about her past. She had been born in Sweet Home, Texas, and had grown up nearby in South

Banks. Some brothers of hers and their families still lived in South Banks, and Lillie spoke often of wanting to visit them and see her parents' graves again. Occasionally Lillie got letters at General Delivery from this place from her brothers—a Marlin and a Tom Perry—or from their families. She showed photographs of them and their children to Buck. He had begun to dread seeing a letter come from one of them, though, because it always made Lillie want to go home. He also had to depend upon her offering to read them to him. When she did so, he suspected that she concealed parts of them. Several times lately Lillie had asked him to give her the money for a bus to go home for a visit. Buck wouldn't hear of it: "That ain't the way for us to do it, Lillie. No, let me take you over there in our camper. Besides, I want to meet your people. They don't never say nothing about me, Buck Lopez, in their letters. . . . " "I've told and retold you Buck, honey. They wouldn't like me coming home that way." Buck sensed that Lillie meant that her family wouldn't approve of her, an Anglo, living with him, a Mexican. Especially not in a camper shell—and unwed too.

"Lillie, *querida*, let's go over there to Texas and get married. Let them see the ceremony. Your brothers could even give you away. . . . " "Oh, Buck, honey. You know I'm already married to Laynie D. Kendricks, Sr., and Rosita is still your legal. . . . " "Listen, Lillie. *Preciosa*, are there any Mexicans . . . I mean Mexican Baptists over near you home in Texas?"

"Of course, silly. South Banks has a growing population of them. Don't you listen when I read you the papers? Didn't you even hear me the other night when I read you that every fifth person in Texas is now a Mexican? Don't you remember how we laughed our sides off because the piece pointed out that the Mexicans are finally taking Texas back?"

"Yeah, I remember. I thought they meant us Mexican Catholics, not Baptists," Buck said weakly. Then winking at Lillie, he added abruptly: "Well, Lillie, you know they used to say back home on the other side that Texas still belongs to Mexico."

"That's just because they've never been willing to admit in the first place that Texas won her independence from them fair and square," Lillie bantered back as she ran her fingers gently through Buck's crew cut.

"What's the matter with you, Lillie? You can live off an old greaser like me, but I'm not good enough to meet your people. No, not even when mine already love you."

"Now, Buck Lopez, remember that despite my Texas independence, I choose to live with you. Besides, honey, there are plenty of Mexican Baptists living over in Texas. More and more of them in South Banks too. Not that there haven't always been some there. Why, haven't I told you about the time my Uncle El baptized a whole bunch of men who came up from Saltillo every summer to help with his peanuts? I was just a girl, but I went to that baptizing on the banks of the river. . . . " And so the matter of their going to Texas together was never settled. Sometimes Buck feared that the reason might be that Lillie was still in love with her husband. After all, he did still live in South Banks. Or maybe it had something to do with one of her three children. He couldn't be sure. Maybe the letters that now came with frequency to General Delivery were either from Laynie D. Kendricks, or else Lillie could be involved in a plan of one kind or another with one of her kids. Anyhow something was up. Buck could tell from the way Lillie's eyes moved as she read the letters that she made up parts of them. The letters weren't always from the person she said they were either. He had begun to study the handwriting on them whenever she was not looking. He had already begun to recognize her daughter Mamie Irene's scrawl. The girl was married to a guy named Jack something or other. They and their kids moved around lots, mostly with a crew of roughnecks, all over Oklahoma and northern Texas.

Buck didn't like the fact that it was only recently that Lillie had admitted she was getting mail from her son, an Eddie Robert Bursanger. She had finally revealed that he was an inmate in the Arizona State Prison at Florence. In vain, Lillie had tried to reason to Buck that she had kept Eddie Robert's presence a secret because she felt that Buck would be ashamed and leave her if he knew she had a son sentenced for life in Florence. So, she swore that, yes, she could tell it had already made a big difference to Buck, because now he had started asking her all those questions about Eddie Robert he knew she couldn't answer. All Lillie would offer Buck in the way of an explanation was to look at him sadly, and say: "Whatever he done, Buck, he done it, because he just couldn't help it. He's just my poor mixed-up baby, that's all. His Daddy never did help him or me any. It's really my fault Eddie Robert's over there in Florence. I just didn't manage things right." Usually

Lillie would break out crying, until Buck silenced her by holding her close. "That's why I want you to keep on being better to your own kids, Buck. After all, you are their Daddy."

Buck would nod and smooth her gray-streaked blonde hair. Yes, he realized, it must have been rough on that boy; on her too. Hadn't Lillie confided to him that Eddie Robert had been born to her during her second marriage to a G.I. from Chicago. The soldier had been stationed near South Banks during W.W.II, and had broken up her first marriage to Mamie Irene's father. Actually, poor Lillie was never legally married to the soldier. It had turned out that he already had a wife and family up in Illinois even before he married her and they began to live together. And Kendricks, Lillie's last husband, had been so mean to Eddie Robert that one of the reasons why she left him was. . . .

"If I ever meet Eddie Robert, then he can call me Dad, Lillie. You know I look on you as my wife, *querida*, and my kids and theirs really do love you. Look how often Timiteo and Margarita and the kids come over here. My kids can be your kids, too, Lillie." But, despite his reassurances, Buck could understand how much she must miss her children

and folks over in Texas. Still he was afraid
of what her son in Florence had done to put
him in prison for life. For this reason, he
never offered to take Lillie to see him. He
was relieved that so far she hadn't asked
him to do so.

Shortly after Lillie had confessed these
things to him, Buck began to see that Lillie
suffered over her son's imprisonment. He
had learned swiftly too that he could not
take Lillie's mind off it by bringing up the
subject of her third and youngest son,
Laynie D. Kendricks, Jr. For although she
took great pride in the fact that Laynie, Jr.,
had landed a scholarship to Baylor University and was becoming a Baptist minister—
her brother Marlin had written her—she
never ceased to long for a letter from the
boy. No, mentioning that youngest one of
Lillie's would only send them to General
Delivery as soon as it opened the next morning. There he would see an even sadder look
come into her searching blue eyes. Yes, it
was better by far to keep Lillie's mind as
much as possible on his own children; but
best of all, on their own ties. "Lillie, when
your uncle El baptized those wetbacks in
the river, and you watched him, was it anything like . . . well, like getting ducked up
and down on the bank of the Rillito on a

Sunday afternoon?" Buck would tease her, not letting up until she laughed so hard he could see her mind was off her troubles.

"Oh, Buck, don't you ever think of anything spiritual?"

"Every time we get together, Lillie."

"Oh, Buck. You big old Mexican rooster you," Lillie would say, burying her head against his white tee shirt.

He liked it best when they were at the shopping center alone together. At such times, when they were safely inside their parking space, they would either stand outside the back door of the camper or walk around the shopping mall. Lillie delighted in the fact that there was both a Goodwill Store and a Yellow Front where they lived. Every time Buck got his social security check, he would take Lillie to one or the other, where she would select some tight new slacks, or a blouse, or a pair of panties. He liked to watch her; she reminded him of that Patricia Neal who played in those late TV movies he used to watch in the bars. She would spend a long time going over each item before she made a selection, talking away to the clerks as she did so. Buck never talked much to them. These days he had even quit asking them about the possibility of a Stylesaver's. Lillie always seemed to be such a trusting person. She never seemed to share Buck's worries that the clerks might alert authorities who could cause them to be run off from their new home. Sometimes at night, if she happened to be standing with him outside their camper when the clerks got off work, Lillie would even wave goodnight. Buck always tried to discourage her by his silence. Still he was concerned that confronting her directly might cause her to leave him. For with Eddie Robert now openly on her mind, Buck knew there was still that danger lurking. Besides, he hated to deny Lillie anything. Nevertheless, sometimes he had to put his foot down. Like recently when she wanted to buy some lawn chairs so they could sit in them beside their camper at night. "No, Lillie, it's just too risky. They might think we are trying to take this place over. Let's play it the safe way, *muchacha mía*."

Nowadays Buck and Lillie had fewer and fewer evenings alone together. Usually Timiteo, his wife Margarita, and their three—Eriquito, Elena Mae, and Baby Tony—would come up in their Ford pickup after Timiteo got off from work in the Baird Bread warehouse. Buck and Lillie would stand beside Timiteo's truck bed and talk to him and Margarita while the kids romped all around the Safeway parking lot. Lillie would usually hold Baby Tony, for whom she had bought at Goodwill, and from her own little savings purse too, a rag monkey. Buck didn't like the way Margarita let Eriquito and Elena Mae run around, skipping and screaming all over the parking lot. He told Timiteo frequently to remind those kids that they weren't in their own back yard. Buck spent much of the visits leading Timiteo around the parking lot after them. As Timiteo chattered about this or that, Buck would lean over and shake each child, whispering: *"Silencio, comprendes?"* Timiteo was too much like his mother, Rosita. Just full of talk and of making babies, and then forgetting them. Privately Buck still held a grudge against Timiteo, since it was he who as his firstborn had pulled him into that youthful, loveless marriage. Buck still remembered his wife as a woman that he and each one of his gang had enjoyed, for back then she seemed to be continually available. It could have been any one of several buddies of his, but he was the one to get trapped with her! Ah well, those other women along the line, they too seemed much the same to him. No, Buck had never been involved with his heart with any of them; no, not the way he had always been with Lillie.

In any case, it was better to have Timiteo and his family around than to have Lillie begging him to let her go off to Texas, or being sad about Eddie Robert up in Florence, or yearning silently for a letter from Laynie, Jr. Buck didn't know whether he should feel happy or sad about the fact that Lillie had been getting to be such good friends with Margarita. He resented it that Lillie was starting to talk more and more to her and to exclude him and Timiteo from the conversation. On the nights Timiteo's family didn't come, some of the other children who now lived away from home came, and always stayed too late. Those younger kids of his had even been thoughtless enough to come visiting him and Lillie on the same night that Timiteo and his family came. It was like a circus with all of them out there together on the parking lot. Buck had finally to tell them not to show up on the same day.

"You oughtn't to tell them anything like that, Buck," Lillie said.

"Now, Lillie, you know a father has to have the say." Then Buck reminded her: "Remember how you're always on me about feeling responsible about my kids and their lives?"

Lately Buck had become increasingly jealous of all his children's and especially his daughter-in-law's devotion to Lillie. Too often now he noticed Lillie talking softly, primarily to her. Always about things he couldn't hear. Meanwhile Margarita and Timiteo's youngsters jabbered away endlessly to him in an unbroken mixture of English and Spanish run together. More and more Buck had been forced to stop listening to the things Timiteo or the grandsons or Elena Mae were trying to tell him, in order to catch what Lillie was saying to Margarita! From time to time, Buck would see Lillie and her looking at photos of Lillie's family. These were photos that Lillie got in letters. One night she even showed Margarita some of the old photos of her children—the ones she used to keep so carefully concealed inside her little purse. Among those photos, he had seen one of the troublesome Eddie Robert as an adolescent: redheaded, curly haired, and with sly blue eyes. Buck hoped and prayed Lillie was not being foolish enough to confide the whereabouts of her son to Margarita. During the recent visits of his children and grandchildren, Buck had tried to stand as close to Lillie as possible, and to keep her continuously involved with the grandchildren and what he too was saying. He tried especially to involve her with Baby Tony and his monkey, for Lillie loved the chubby tyke best of all the children.

"Oh, Tony Boy; you're just like my Laynie, Jr., when he was your size! Yes, Baby Dumpling; oh, yes, you are," Lillie would say, often burying her head and nose in the tummy of the giggling toddler. Buck knew this was the greatest compliment Lillie could pay any child. It delighted him when he could manipulate her into saying it over and over again to Tony. When Margarita and Timiteo asked to see a picture of Laynie, Jr., Lillie had just nodded her head, tears catching at the corner of her eyes. "I don't have a one," she said. "No, not a one. His Daddy's mother . . . she took away every one when she took him away from me. . . . Yes, every single one. Why, I ain't even seen my baby since he was three years old."

So deeply touched was Timiteo upon hearing this that he went over and put his arm around Lillie. Then he kissed her on the cheek. The next time Timiteo came by for a visit, he had surprised Buck by bringing Lillie a chocolate cake from Bairds'. After presenting the gift, and while he and

Buck were walking around the parking lot together in pursuit of Eriquito and Elena Mae, Timiteo said: "Listen, Pappa, why don't you buy Lillie a ticket over to Texas, so she can visit with her folks? You know she ought to see her son Laynie, Jr., after all these years. She could fly over and back as cheap on West Saver Airlines as she could go by bus. She'd save time too. And you could stay with us while she was gone. Margarita could even get Mama to send the two youngest kids over to our house to visit with you. They keep begging me to come over here and see you, and even Mama doesn't seem to even mind."

Buck told Timiteo to mind his own business.

"I know, Pappa. It just isn't the safe way," Timiteo said, winking.

"No, it isn't," Buck nodded. "And you, you smart alec, you better respect Lillie and me. And so had those two kids of mine who still live with your Mama. You tell them that Lillie is Pappa's . . . well, like his wife. You understand me?" Buck said, suddenly remembering the trouble Rosita could cause over the use of the word "wife."

Summer was ending. One evening when Timiteo was visiting, Buck said: "We sure do need a heater in the camper if we stay in

Tucson all year, and we'd like to."

"No problem, Pappa. I got this buddy who has a power lawn mower. He'd probably be willing to rent it to you so that you could earn a little extra money doing some yard work. That way you could buy the little panel ray heater that we saw on special the other night at the Checker Auto Parts."

"Oh Buck, wouldn't it be great if we could afford it. You know now that Margarita is expecting again, I could spend the time you are out working over there with her and help her take care of these children, especially Baby Tony," Lillie called out. Then she walked over to join the men, with Margarita smiling and following her lead.

"We'd just love having you over there with us, wouldn't we, guys?" Margarita told the youngsters who were nodding and jockeying for attention around the group.

"You bet'cha," Timiteo said. "And you really do need a heater in that camper badly during the winter months. Last year, I have to admit we worried that you might not get to come as often as you did because of all that cold weather we kept having down here."

But Buck didn't promise at first. He gave the matter considerable thought for a day or so, and talked it over with Lillie. When he could see that she really wanted to stay on in Tucson, he decided that he would start mowing at once. All things considered, it was probably the best plan for Lillie to spend the time he was away at Timiteo's house. Maybe that way she'd get tired of her perpetual chatter with Margarita. Maybe it would take her mind off her own kids over in Texas, and she'd see how lucky her life in the camper was once she put in a day of chasing those three all around Timiteo's house.

When Buck returned to mowing the lawns around Tucson, he was reminded of the torture of those early days of knowing Lillie. Here he was again, despite his retirement, back doing the yard work, with Lillie so much on his mind that sometimes his customer would tell him, when they paid him for a day's work, that he needn't come back again.

At night, even when he was trying to make love to Lillie, he noticed how much she talked about silly things, like what Margarita—or even Elena Mae—said. Yes, the kid too. These days he didn't dare work late on any job, not even when a lawn badly needed mowing. For if he did so, he would find some of his younger children over at Margarita's visiting with Lillie, and he would have to stay late himself, so as not to disappoint them.

Buck had hoped too that his children's visits to the parking lot would cease, at least while he was undertaking the yard work. To his dismay, however, he saw that Lillie encouraged them to come over as much as possible. And when they visited, more and more Lillie seemed absorbed in conversations with Margarita, all of which excluded him. There was too much giggling between them. Little or no attention paid to the grandchildren. Worst of all, only those kids vied for Buck's attention. Meanwhile here was Timiteo endlessly running his mouth off about the guys at Bairds' and their women.

To top it off, Lillie hadn't wanted to go down to the Rillito River bed with Buck for two weekends now. It had always been their custom on Saturdays and Sundays to drive down there to an out-of-the-way spot they knew behind some palo verde trees so that in the daylight passersby would not see the camper shaking. Even when it was raining, and going to the river was out of the question, they would go to some unfrequented corner of a city park. It wasn't risky really because most people were indoors. But it wasn't just weekends that were wasted any more. Nowadays on week nights, his children visited them so late after work, he did not have time to sleep enough, much less satisfy his continuous desire. For despite his fatigue, the urge was increasing so that he was all but having to force Lillie. It perplexed him that this was perhaps the reason that she did not want to go to the river bed, the reason she begged him instead to go over to be more with Baby Tony. "You ought to know your grandchildren better, Buck. You're missing out on a lot there, I can tell you," Lillie scolded.

"No, it's you who are missing out on the big thing," he would say, inviting her to bed. To his chagrin, Lillie would look away and peer outside the camper window. More than once, he muttered and tried to insist, but it was seldom to any avail. Or else he'd scowl and openly show his anger. But that never seemed to help either. So he would give up for the time being, realizing that in a few hours he would only be wanting her badly again. Things had to change.

By the third week of his yard work, despite his preoccupation with Lillie, Buck had saved up almost enough money for the heater. At the end of the week, he had made up his mind he would not undertake any more jobs. It was several months before All Souls'

but he was going to take Lillie down to
Sasabe, away from all these pesky problems. She had always enjoyed that place
with him. He would take her to the quiet
nook down there, and they would do nothing but satisfy themselves. Even in daylight,
and all afternoon if they wanted. In Sasabe,
he would really bring the old Lillie back.
And maybe after that, they would start
traveling again. He could see now that not
only he, but Lillie, too, needed to be saved
from all the problems that came from being
settled and tied down. Yes, he must take her
away as soon as possible in the camper. It
would be better to live on the run for awhile
than like this. Maybe they could flee first to
Phoenix, where it was warmer, and live
near a Safeway there. Owens didn't seem to
matter now. For in reality, Buck could see
that it wasn't the lack of caring for one's
children and their needs, or the involvement
in social necessities that saved a relationship. It was simply the need for the man
and woman involved to continue com-
municating their own needs. After all, that
was what everyone—all souls—needed.
Maybe Lillie wasn't such a great housewife.
Still what her real problem was that she was
such a great mother, and being great that
way, had nothing to do with being a good

But it was already too late. On the way over, they heard on the pick-up radio that just outside of Benson, Eddie Robert Bursanger had shot to death an older unidentified female companion who was traveling with him, and then killed himself. Buck fainted when he heard the announcement.

When Buck came to, he found himself in Kino Hospital in Tucson, where he had been undergoing treatment for several days for severe shock. As he regained consciousness, he learned from Timiteo all that had transpired while he had been under sedation. Through her brothers over in South Banks, Texas, the police had identified Lillie as Eddie Robert's mother. The brothers had been listed in the police records as both Eddie Robert's and Lillie's next of kin. They had arranged for her and her son's funerals the day before in her hometown. Timiteo had been in touch with them by phone and had told them and the police, too, that his father was hospitalized and in a state of shock over Lillie's death. He had asked the brothers to arrange with a florist in South Banks for a casket wreath of roses for Lillie from the Lopez family, with a banner across it saying: "Beloved Wife and Mother."

From the brothers and the newspapers the story of why Eddie Robert had killed Lillie had emerged. According to the papers, police records showed that Eddie Robert had tried to kill Lillie before. That had happened six years ago, at the same time that he had killed the owner of a Phoenix bar—a man with whom it was rumored Lillie had been living at the time. But the records also showed that over and over, both to a judge and a jury, Lillie had continuously denied that Eddie Robert had attempted to kill her when he shot the bar owner. It was said though that she had never been able to convince the others of the truth of her convictions, and now people could see why. For, as soon as Lillie's brothers learned of her death at her son's hand, they made public the fact that Eddie Robert had hated Lillie all his life.

Lillie's brothers said that the boy had always blamed Lillie for not being married to his father, and for not bringing him up among his father's people. He imagined them as people of an upper class society into which Lillie didn't fit. In truth, neither the kid's father nor any of his relations on that side had expressed any desire ever to see him, much less have anything to do with him. Eddie Robert had found that out more than once when he had gone up to Illinois to see them and had been turned away.

The way Lillie's brothers saw it, Lillie had always felt guilty about her son's hatred of her, and had always indulged him in his every whim. Lately, she had written them that she had, among other reasons, been staying on in the Tucson area so as to be near him. She still insisted he was innocent, and had written them that he was certain to be granted parole. She begged them to forgive him when that happened and to let him bring her home for a visit. In her letters these past few months, Lillie had been insisting that she wanted to talk with them about a lot of "important changes in her life which had been taking place," so many of which, she always wrote, "would please them." They didn't know what these changes were since now Lillie was dead and couldn't tell them.

But now that they had heard from Timiteo about his dad, they realized Lillie must have wanted to tell them about her marriage to his father and their new life together. Still, they wondered why she had kept the news such a secret, especially since she must have known that they were aware of the fact that she had divorced Laynie D. Kendricks a while back. Kendricks had told

them about the divorce and was already re-
married himself. Timiteo had only told the
brother that he couldn't say what Lillie's
reasons might have been, but assured them
of Buck's and his children's devotion to her.
The brothers had seemed pleased even
though they sounded over the phone to be
rather distant-acting Texas *gringos*.

From the moment Buck heard the news
from Timiteo that he was now considered
Lillie's husband in her hometown and by
her own kin, he began to regain his strength
swiftly and to plan for his trip over to Texas
in his camper. Timiteo had paved the way.
His mother, Rosita, would never know that
way over there in South Banks, Texas, Buck
was looked on at this very moment as Lillie's husband.

From the beginning of his new life in South
Banks, Buck spent most of his time working
on Lillie's grave, keeping his camper nearby
in the rundown cemetery parking lot. In
fact, he was seen so much in the place that
the mayor of the small town soon called
upon him and offered him the job of being
the caretaker there. For years, the city had
not been able to find a good steady worker
for that job. But the mayor told Buck, as he
signed him on the city payroll, that he be-

lieved he might be just the man they needed. So Buck soon had a job, which not only offered him the opportunity to live legally in the cemetery, but also promised him enough money to purchase a nice headstone for Lillie's grave. At the same time, he could still keep his social security check, which allowed him to earn the small salary the new job paid.

Once he had been in South Banks for a few days, it had become apparent to Buck that everyone truly considered him as Lillie's surviving husband. He was so pleased in his new role that he did not even worry about his legal ties to Rosita any more. No, not especially when he had chanced to learn that the whole town looked upon Laynie D. Kendricks, Sr., as a former husband of Lillie's anyway. Though Buck now realized that Kendricks must have committed bigamy some months before in order to marry a local widow with a new oil well, Buck felt confident that Kendricks would not likely ever be questioning his claim to being Lillie's last husband. No, it seemed, in fact, that Kendricks was lending some unexpected aid in confirming Buck's right to the title. For Buck had heard that Kendricks, who had remained close friends with Lillie's brothers, had convinced them that

Lillie had divorced him a while back. Nowadays he was saying that it must be apparent to them too that she really divorced him in order to marry Buck Lopez. It seemed too that Lillie's son, Laynie, Jr., as well as her daughter, Mamie Irene, were under the same impression though they both lived away and he hadn't met either of them.

Most of all Buck took pride in the obituary that had appeared in *The South Banks Weekly Times*. The florist had given him a copy of it when he went by the shop to pay for Lillie's casket wreath. He thanked her and put it in the hip pocket of his jeans until he could return to the cemetery where he got one of the Mexican grave diggers working out there to read it over and over to him until he knew it by heart. The obituary noted that "Mrs. Lillie Perry Lopez was survived by her husband, Johnny (Buck) Lopez, Sr., of Tucson, a son, the Rev. Laynie D. Kendricks, Jr., of Waco, a daughter, Mamie Irene (Mrs. Jack) Jackson of Tulsa, eight step-children in Arizona, nine grandchildren in Oklahoma and Arizona, two sisters, Billie Lucille Whitcomb of Sweet Home, Texas, and Mamie Joyce Dexter of Fort Worth, and by her brothers, Marlin A. and Tom B. Perry of South Banks." The obituary went on to say that "before Mrs. Lopez had been shot to death by her eldest son, Eddie Robert Bursanger, who had taken his own life shortly afterwards, she had been living with her husband, Buck Lopez, in Tucson. Since Lopez's retirement from rodeo work in Arizona, he and Mrs. Lopez had spent most of their time traveling around the state seeing places of historic interest. For the past six months, however, they had been living in Tucson in order to be near Lopez's children and grandchildren by a previous marriage."

The report of his marriage to Lillie in the local newspaper was second only to the wedding license he had so long desired. In fact, the obituary, erroneous as it was, was really the official document that gave him the incentive to face the empty days ahead. It was what had made him actually decide to remain in South Banks, live in his camper, and work toward beautifying Lillie's grave. The job now as caretaker was more good fortune than he could ever have bargained for.

As Buck rode the cemetery power mower or cleaned off the various graves by hand, his one ambition became that of buying for Lillie's grave a pink granite marker of the kind that matched the Texas capitol over at

Austin. She had told him over and over that she thought it was one of the most beautiful buildings on earth, and as he worked in the cemetery he often saw similar markers of this native stone. He wanted to buy the stone and have it put in place so that Lillie could see it when she returned to earth on the first All Souls' Day after her death. The date was approaching, and for this reason he worked so hard at the cemetery, and helped so often in the digging of new graves, that he overtaxed himself and had to see a doctor. The doctor warned him that he had a heart problem and should slow down. At the same time, Buck became aware that he was earning the townspeople's respect, for people stopped to thank him for the miracle he was working on their burial place. Those who had known Lillie or her parents, Abner and Irene Perry, told him, as they expressed sympathy in his recent loss, that he was making both his wife's and his in-law's graves the cemetery's most inviting resting places. Even Lillie's brothers, who had barely acknowledged his presence in South Banks, much less visited him in the cemetery, were heard saying to townspeople: "Yep, it's true that on the last go around, Lillie married herself a Mexican. But now, let me tell you, he's the kind that knows how to work. Why, that old boy was a well-known bronc-buster out in Arizona before him and Lillie retired. And you know how they say a Mexican's just a natural-born caretaker; well, any one can see there's truth to that saying anytime they go out to the marble orchard and watch Lillie's old man working it over."

Buck had also been warmly received at the St. Ignatius Catholic Church, where each Sunday he was present at early mass. There were Mexican parishioners, as well as Anglos of every class, who tried to make him feel at home and to become better friends with him. At first, Buck kept mostly to himself. It was shortly after his caretaker job began that he became better and better friends with a retired and senile priest of Czech descent named Father Severin Locavek. A forgotten old man without relatives, the priest had returned to his home town so that he could be buried beside his parents. He lived in the one rest home in the town, and was delighted by the attention Buck paid him. He loved to go to the cemetery where he was one day scheduled to rest. After mass, with more and more frequency, Buck took him out there, and kept him there all day too, saying prayers over Lillie's grave as well as those of the priest's own

127

parents. It wasn't long until Buck shortened his name and began, with affection, to call him "Father Loco."

As Buck listened to the priest's jumbled, crazed stories about events past and present in South Banks, and in return told him about his love and devotion to his wife Lillie, he began to realize that the priest, in his senility, made little distinction between the dead and the living. Buck thought that was a marvelous way to be, and felt freer and freer to talk with him about Lillie as though she were still living. Buck found himself rejoicing the first time he saw Father Loco standing before Lillie's grave and talking to it as though Lillie were a living person. After that Buck enjoyed Father Loco's company even more, because he was now able to include Lillie openly in their get-togethers and to such an extent that the priest seemed to feel her presence and try to visit with her too. For this reason, Buck kept him out at the cemetery as long as possible on Sundays, only returning him at the last moment to the rest home, and always full of chile, cheeseburgers, and Gallo wine. One day Buck discovered to his genuine delight that the priest's favorite subject was how to practice good marital relationships and a healthy sex life in a Catholic household.

Sometimes the priest got so tipsy on the Gallo wine that he preached sermons on the subject out among the tombstones. It made Buck especially gregarious when the priest included advice for him and the ever-present Lillie. Buck would fill his wine glass again on hearing it, and try to coax the old man into repeating it over and over.

One day just a few weeks before All Souls', Buck got a call from Timiteo at the cemetery office, which was really just a shed for the power mower and yard equipment. Rosita had died earlier that day. Timiteo was wondering if Buck, for the sake of the younger children, would like to borrow the money from him and some of the other kids, to fly home for the funeral. No, Buck told him. For Lillie's sake, he could not. It would not look good, especially now when everyone looked on him over in Texas as Lillie's legal husband. Besides, he wanted his other children by Rosita, just as Timiteo showed he did, to look upon him in the same way. It was just risking too much. For Timiteo's and his other children's sake, he would pay for Rosita's funeral, instead, and also send his youngest child the money so that he could come over and visit him during the Christmas holidays. Maybe if the boy liked Texas he could move over there and live with Buck too. He expressed his sympathy to Timiteo and the others, but he admitted before he hung up that he did know a new relief now in being a legally free man. Once again he cautioned Timiteo never to tell others, especially not Lillie's family, the facts. None of them need ever know now that he had never been able to marry Lillie before a priest because his church vows to Rosita had kept him from doing so. Timiteo assured him he understood, and promised before he told his father goodbye, that for the sake of all concerned he would continue to keep his secret.

When Buck put down the phone, he rushed over to the rest home and asked Father Loco if he would marry Lillie and him in an early evening ceremony on All Souls' Day. During his lucid moments, the priest seemed to think that the marriage ceremony would be some kind of renewal of vows that former parishioners of his used to request for special anniversaries of theirs. But most of the time in his senility he seemed to think of Lillie as a young, living bride. Without any kind of hesitation, he agreed to officiate on All Souls' Night, and, to Buck's amazement, even began to talk to Lillie and him as though they were a prospective, youthful bride and groom.

So it was that at 7 p.m. on All Souls' Night, and by candles which lit the pathway up to Lillie's grave and surrounded the large granite marker, newly fixed there, that Buck Lopez finally stood before a real priest and married Lillie Perry. For Buck had never doubted that Lillie would return to earth on that night, nor that she was standing beside him, before the marker, as they said their vows. He had known this would be Lillie's choice for a wedding night; she looked as pretty as that Patricia Neal did in some of those good old movies; and she was dressed up even prettier than the nice way she used to dress when they would go down to Sasabe to see his mother annually on this night. Buck was just certain that Lillie could see the bridal bouquet of twelve red roses he had ordered from the florist's, the boutonniere he wore in his new black serge suit. Maybe since he had dressed up like this she would tell him again, like she did in the early days, that he still looked like Anthony Quinn. In any case, she was certain to a enjoy the good Texas homecooking— the spicy combination plate of delicious Mexican food and the cup of strong black coffee he had gotten the Bluebonnet Cafe to prepare for her at the same time they made up take-out orders for Father Loco and him.

Surely, Lillie could see the huge platter of food awaiting her in the aluminum foil container. It reflected the tall candles nearby and the long stemmed glass of Gallo wine. Buck intended to refill Lillie's glass each time he filled his own. Most of all he was anxious for Lillie to discover the hymnal from the First Baptist Church. It lay in the center of her grave with one white lily placed across the cover. One of the Mexican grave digger friends who had grown up a Baptist in the region had brought the hymnal to Buck from Lillie's old church to use for a week or two. Buck had told his friend that he wanted to borrow it to learn some of Lillie's favorite hymns, especially "When the Roll Is Called Up Yonder." His friend had brought the book to him first thing the next morning. He had also eagerly extended to Buck a personal invitation from his pastor, Brother Jerry Bob Slayton, who had conducted Lillie's funeral services, to be present at his wife's church the next Sunday morning. Brother Slayton had promised that the song would be sung at that time following his baptism of some new members. He would also like for Buck to come to the potluck dinner his congregation was serving on the church grounds immediately following the services.

At the wedding on All Souls' Night, Buck knew that he had been very wise to ask Father Loco to officiate. For, when the priest turned toward the headstone asking Lillie to repeat her vows, he seemed to accept Buck's answers as natural: to represent Lillie's own voice coming out to him there in the candlelight. After all, since Father Loco had never actually seen Lillie in person, but had heard Buck talk constantly to and about her in all their visits together, Lillie seemed to be an ever-present companion, who best lived in Buck's voice anyhow. So, at the wedding service, Father Loco simply addressed the headstone and Buck like they were an ordinary couple standing before him in one of the small Czech farming community churches where he had married more people than he could now remember. At the end of the ceremony, when Buck put his arms around a part of the new tombstone which marked the head of Lillie's grave and lovingly kissed the name upon it, the priest laid one hand upon the top of the stone and the other on Buck's head. Then, he blessed the couple as though both were living presences before him. Afterwards, at Buck's insistence, the old priest got on his knees, and as he peered through his wire-framed glasses, read the words carved on the double headstone aloud to the new groom: "Here lie Mr. and Mrs. Buck Lopez." On Lillie's side of the divided marker, he read: "Lillie Irene Perry," with "Beloved wife of Buck Lopez," below the first line of Lillie's names and above her birth and death dates. On the side adjacent to Lillie's, he read: "Johnny B. ("Buck") Lopez, Sr.," with the words: "Pvt., Ret., U.S. Army Cavalry, W.W.II," below the name, with only the birth date given below the army rank.

As Father Loco and Buck celebrated around the Lopez family headstone on two bottles of Gallo, it seemed to the old priest that the wedding had taken place a long time ago. As the old man, along with Buck who seemed forever tending Lillie's glass, got drunker and drunker, from time to time he sang "When the Roll Is Called Up Yonder." As Buck listened to the priest's slurred singing, he weaved back and forth before Lillie's headstone, saying: "I just had to marry you, Lillie, darling. You know, *cariño mío*, it's the safe way now that we're together once again on All Souls'." Then he would laugh wildly. When he was not singing, the Father talked loudly, his pronounced Czech accent becoming thicker and thicker, as he spoke to the newlyweds upon his favorite subject: "Utilizing Rhythm and Birth Control"— a sermon Buck kept calling "The Safe Way to Satisfaction."

Around midnight, Buck Lopez had a heart attack and died at once. The tired old priest, already passed out from drunkenness, was unaware all night that the companion stretched nearby was resting eternally. The priest was hospitalized the next morning when some early visitors to the cemetery had discovered him there, again singing "When the Roll Is Called Up Yonder" in a semi-senile and decidedly drunken stupor. At the same time, the visitors had found the body of Buck Lopez slumped against Lillie's grave with a wine glass in each hand and the trace of a smile on his lips.

* * * * * *

LaVerne Harrell Clark, a native of Smithville, Texas, is the author of four books of nonfiction and photography. Her short stories have appeared in literary magazines and anthologies. Three of those included in *The Deadly Swarm and Other Stories* have received awards, the most recent of which is the 1984 Julian Ocean Literature Prize. Also a folklorist and photographer of Native Americans, she has traveled and researched extensively in Mexico, Spain, and the southwestern United States. For this work she has received the University of Chicago Folklore Award, a grant from the American Philosophical Society, and other prestigious prizes. A graduate of Texas Woman's University, LaVerne Harrell Clark holds an M.A. from the University of Arizona, where she is currently enrolled in the M.F.A. program. She has worked with Vance Bourjaily, Francine Prose, and Angus Wilson, and at Columbia University with John R. Humphreys. The founding and former director of the University of Arizona Poetry Center, LaVerne Harrell Clark now lives in Tucson with her husband, novelist and literary critic L.D. Clark.